HELLYER'S TRIP

HELLYER'S TRIP

AN ESPIONAGE NOVEL

Philip Prowse

Kernel Books

First published in Great Britain in 2018 by Kernel Books.

Kernel Books
7 Camaret Drive
St Ives
Cornwall
TR26 2BE

kernelbooks.com

Copyright © 2018 by Philip Prowse

Typeset by Design for Writers in Adobe Garamond Pro.

The moral right of Philip Prowse to be identified as the author of this work has been asserted in accordance with the Copyright, Designs and Patents Act, 1988.

A CIP catalogue record for this book is available from the British Library.

ISBN 978 1 5272 0935 0

For Rhiannon

The Alexandrians themselves were strangers and exiles to the Egypt which existed below the glittering surface of their dreams.

– Lawrence Durrell, *Mountolive*

PROLOGUE

Alexandria, Egypt, 5 June 1967

At midnight on the first day of the Six Day War, Lieutenant Commander Abraham Dror eases the Israeli submarine *Tanin* through the defences of Alexandria's Western Harbour and brings it to rest on the seabed.

Six frogmen from the elite Shayetet 13 unit swim out of the torpedo tubes and head for their targets: two Egyptian Z-class destroyers, moored at buoys opposite the breakwater. The divers locate the vessels, attach limpet mines to the hulls and return to the underwater rendezvous point.

But the *Tanin* has slipped out to sea.

Oxygen cylinders running low, the frogmen head for shore. As they climb on to the jumble of rocks by Fort Quait Bey they hear the deep rumble of explosions from the mined vessels. The Israelis celebrate, unaware that the Egyptian Navy now rotates berths after dusk. Their achievement has been to sabotage a dredger and a supply barge.

Four are caught cowering in rock crevices at dawn and later the other two, walking jauntily along the Corniche in rumpled T-shirts and shorts, are spotted by an alert fifteen-year-old.

All are incarcerated in Ras-El-Tin naval prison. The thunder of boots and clang of cell doors heralding their arrival drags Nick Hellyer back into painful consciousness.

CHAPTER 1

'MY, THAT WAS A soft landing.'
She climbed off.

Slim figure hidden in an embroidered magenta fringed kaftan and tie-dyed jeans, eyes dark with mascara and mischief.

'Couple of tabs?'

'Why?'

'Say sorry I crashed on you.'

Multi-coloured worms on the great white drop sheet hanging from the hall balcony throbbed to the threatening organ-led rhythms of The Crazy World of Arthur Brown.

Until that coming-together, Nick had lain at peace with himself, cruciform, staring up at the mirror ball with its fractured images of people variously dancing, leaping and prancing, getting off on erotic movies, debating macrobiotics in cross-legged circles, snipping the clothes off a willing teenage girl under the instruction of a black-clad performance artist, smoking banana skins in the forlorn hope of a high, or dope with a more certain chance of success.

Peaceful, less from being stoned and more from not being there – Cambridge, that claustrophobic Fenland university populated by public-school boys, sailing on, blissfully unaware of the impending wave of change that would engulf it.

Here, he could will on unexpected eventualities. Here, in the haze of incense, the performance artist could really have been Yoko Ono, and it had actually been Andy Warhol cruising outside in the silver Rolls Royce. Here, a sky-borne dancer had just smothered him in long blonde hair as she crashed over his legs, mid-twirl.

'Acid? I've never—'

'You know – do or die. And you can call me Bex.'

'Nick.'

'Good boy, Nick. Tongue out now. Swallow.'

As the opening chords of Pink Floyd's 'See Emily Play' bounced off yellow brick walls, waves of strobe lights flowed over him and his legs slowly took on a life of their own, jigging restlessly.

'Babe, wanna dance?'

'Not yet. Know what I'm talking about. Come with me.'

Taking his hand, she led him to a dimmer corner where people lay on mattresses alone, or in couples or threes, some lost to the world, others exploring their own inner and outer worlds.

White-sleeved arms and denim-clad legs waved and glided through the incense-laden atmosphere. An intense awareness kicked in. Dancers came into focus, then blurred out again.

With a gentle half-smile, head tilted to one side, Bex unbuttoned the front of her kaftan and held it open with both hands. Firm flat breasts, outlined by target-like concentric blue rings, lurked behind the curtain of long blonde hair.

'Relax, lie flat and close your eyes. Feel the vibe with me, man.'

Straddling him, Bex stroked a sticky gel into his hair and beard, making him giggle. She rolled off and caught his hand.

'Let it dry.'

Expert fingers loosened his jeans, a warm mouth descended and silky hair brushed across his thighs as both kaleidoscope and cacophony faded away. Blurry eyes opened to a vision of Bex running her tongue around her lips before swallowing.

'Now, my turn.'

'Go on then.'

The Floyd pulsated through his head as he unzipped her Levi's to slip an eager exploring forefinger inside.

What the fuck?

A small, hard cock and balls.

A fully equipped guy who had just sucked him off. Now expecting him to return the compliment.

He ripped out his hand and lurched back against the wall, seeking support against the whirlwind.

'No. Can't. Sorry. Nothing personal. Got to get back to Cambridge now. Just not my scene.'

Bex slithered across the floor to recline forgivingly beside him.

'Sure, man, whatever turns you on. Cambridge, eh? Funnily enough, best mate of mine there's expecting something from me. Tell you what – you can take it. Save posting. Sort of make things up to me. Know what I mean? What train you going on?'

'Milk train. First one from Liverpool Street.'

They tramped in silence through ill-lit slippery streets to the station, where the dregs of Cambridge undergraduate society awaited. White-caped, dinner-jacketed party animals cheered as in succession they relieved themselves over the edge of the platform. Unconcerned, Bex sought out a payphone and, on his return, pulled a paperback-sized package from a deep pocket in his kaftan.

'Here. My mate Angel will be there when you get in – he'll know who you are.'

'How?'

'Don't worry, he will.'

***

A PROLONGED WHISTLE DROVE him hurtling half-awake towards the carriage door, only to dash back for the package before it was carried off to Ely. Dazed, he headed first in the wrong direction down Cambridge's endless single platform but, hearing his name called, turned back to see an arm waving.

'Hi, brother. I'm Angel. Got the stuff?'

'Here. From Bex.'

A firm tap on his right shoulder.

'Just a minute, sir.'

CID warrant card in his face. Another detective taking the package from Angel and leading him away.

'Why on earth?'

'Possession of marijuana with an intent to supply will do for a start, sir.'

'I haven't the faintest idea what you're talking about. Luke's College can vouch for me.'

'That's as may be, sir. But your college authorities could well change their minds when they see you in the flesh.'

'Sorry?'

'Well, you young gentlemen of the university might think it amusing to refer to us as the boys in blue. But this time I think we've caught Little Boy Blue.'

Turning his head, Nick caught sight of his reflection in a carriage window. His dark hair and beard were now a brilliant, startling blue.

Suppressing an overpowering urge to giggle, he allowed himself to be handcuffed and pushed into the back of a car for the short drive to the police station in Regent Street.

'Name and address? Empty your pockets. Shoelaces and belt.'

'Can I make a call, please?'

'Not now, sonny. Nine o'clock.'

The desk sergeant led him to a white-tiled cell and the mutterings of a malodorous vagrant, the snoring of a middle-aged man in a red-wine-stained business suit, and the grunts of two overly cocky arm-wrestling teenagers.

Head buzzing with shock, but irrationally secure in the certainty that it would all be sorted out soon, he lay back on a wooden bench.

'Let's be having you, Little Boy Blue. Telephone time.'

For once that day his luck was in, as he got straight through to Dr Fuller, the dean of Luke's College. Little consolation was to be had.

'This is most unfortunate, Hellyer, and no mistake. Doesn't look good at all, I'm afraid. But I'll see what we can do. If they do let you out, come straight here to see me.'

Two hours later the yawning desk sergeant obliged.

'Right, you can leave. You're on bail until a hearing at the next magistrates' court. And you can thank your lucky stars that your damned college has so much influence. Now get out.'

As he entered Luke's, Jackson, the famously discreet head porter, could not resist a raised eyebrow.

'Suits you, sir.'

He reddened, only to be confronted by James, with whom he shared a set of rooms in college.

'What's up with you?'

'Can't stop. Late. Summoned to see Sam.'

'Judging by your *dramatic* appearance, you're due for a bollocking.'

Dr Fuller, always addressed by surname and title but always referred to as Sam, nursed a legendary antipathy for university theatricals. Rumour had it he'd been a brigadier in Military Intelligence in the Second World War, and still retained active links to the secret world.

The inner door to Sam's set of rooms hung open, and Nick gave a polite cough as he entered. In a green leather swivel chair, sideways to a huge roll-top desk, sat a heavy figure in a capacious Prince of Wales check three-piece suit, the waistcoat dotted with fallen snuff. Sam removed his monocle and his frighteningly clear blue eyes fell upon Nick.

'Ah, Hellyer, you reported being in a spot of bother, and judging from your ghastly appearance that would most certainly seem to be the case. Not to beat about the bush, I may be able to help you, and you may be able to be of assistance to your country. Do I make my meaning clear?'

Although capable of processing the surface meaning of the words, Nick failed to detect any deeper significance. Sam had not offered him a chair, so he stood with his hands held stiffly by his sides.

'Not exactly, sir.'

The dean's jowls quivered.

'Must I spell it out? I'm offering you a way out of your pre-dicament. As things stand you'll be tried and, when sentenced, receive a substantial prison term – I believe the tariff is at least seven years. Of course, the college would have nothing to do with you in that circumstance.'

'I—'

'Hear me out. I'd also imagine that, as a convicted drug dealer, you'd find it exceedingly difficult to continue your academic career elsewhere in these islands. Do you compre-hend fully?'

'Yes, sir.'

'Now it so happens that I'm tasked by friends in high places to propose suitable young men. You're not unknown to me by any means – or indeed to my friends. Truth be told, they've had a very good look at you already, on my recommendation.'

'But—'

'In due course, you would have been approached and, I would hope, successfully recruited. What you've just related to me dramatically changes that scenario. If you wish, I can pass on news of your changed circumstances and immediate availability. However, I don't have the last word.'

'I'm sorry, Dr Fuller, I'm really not sure what you're sug-gesting. What does it involve doing?'

'Lying for your country, Hellyer.'

The shadow of a grin passed over Sam's features.

'Not as a diplomat – that takes years to perfect – but as someone undercover, someone who's not what they seem. You'll pursue your academic career overseas, while also under-taking certain other duties. If you agree, I'll make a telephone call. Depending on the result, you may leave for London at once where you'll be interviewed and vetted. What happens after that depends on operational needs, but I'd reckon on quite a long period overseas after training.'

'Training? For what, sir? I already have a doctorate.'

'Yes, but you'd surely admit that you're not exactly under-cover material yet.'

'But what about all the mess here?'

'Once your potential new role is explained at the appropri-ate level, the police will have no further immediate interest in you. The charge may remain on their books, but will not be actively pursued. Now, shall I make that call?'

'Yes, sir.'

'Very well, and do take a seat.'

The dean levered himself out of the swivel chair and lum-bered across to his bedroom, pulling the heavy cream door to behind him. He reappeared ten minutes later.

'Hellyer, they'll see you.'

'Thank you, sir.'

'Now be off with you, young man. Clean out your rooms and leave your trunk at the porter's lodge. I don't advise trying to explain your departure to your girlfriend, or indeed any friends – we'll put about a rumour involving admission to Fulbourn Mental Hospital.'

Sam lowered his head for a moment, then raised it, his seemingly innocent blue eyes boring straight into Nick.

'In a way I envy you, my boy. Most people have one life in front of them, but you have two. For good, or for evil. Think about that.'

'Yes, Dr Fuller.'

'Right, now. Practicalities: this is where you're to present yourself tomorrow morning at eight a.m., and here is where you'll stay tonight.'

Nick accepted the two cards.

'Now, be gone. And, for God's sake, do something about that blasted hair of yours.'

***

BLUE DYE SWIRLED AROUND the plughole of his bedroom hand basin, disappearing as surely as his Cambridge career would. He chose those of his sketches he most liked and stowed them in his trunk with his clothes and academic papers. He packed a suit, shirt and tie into a soft brown leather bag and set off for the B&B in Sussex Gardens to which Sam had directed him.

Staring out into the darkness from the London train, he folded his arms tightly over his shoulders in search of comfort.

***

THE NEXT MORNING, FORMALLY dressed and rather more self-possessed, he presented himself at a mews building near King Charles Street. After he'd rung several times, a stiff-faced woman in a brown overall admitted him.

'May be a while – often is.'

As he perched in the cramped foyer, his confidence gradually drained into the shiny toecaps of his shoes. An hour and a flight of narrow stairs later, he entered an office whose uniformed occupant leapt to his feet and thrust a large sweaty palm over the file-cluttered desk.

'Patrick Quinlevan. Good to put a face to a name, Hellyer. Do apologise for keeping you waiting. We already know a considerable amount about you, but I'd better warn you that I'm going to put you through the wringer now – expect you've heard of positive vetting.'

Nick had not.

Major Quinlevan's oiled-down wiry black hair looked as if it might spring up at any moment and take on a life of its own. An air of guileless enthusiasm shone from his face.

For the next three hours, he grilled Nick about his life history: not only education and work, but also friends, family, foreign travel, cultural interests, political affiliation and opinions, sexual orientation, and career ambitions.

'Cross-referenced with others, of course – but they were mostly unaware of the purpose of our enquiries.'

After filling out detailed health and lifestyle questionnaires at his early-afternoon medical, his knees were tapped and his lungs listened to. He removed his shirt for three chest X-Rays, gave a urine sample and waited patiently to be interviewed.

The doctor, a kind, resigned woman with well-bitten fingernails, took him through his questionnaires, then interrogated him about his sexual history. His answers omitted any reference to Bex.

Finally, he returned to Quinlevan.

'Capital! Should have all the results in the morning.'

***

CURIOUS AS TO WHAT lay ahead, and in the belief that the previous day had gone well, he entered the major's office with a purposeful stride, only to be brought up short.

Alone in the room stood a woman in her early sixties, with a helmet of close-cut white hair and the bearing of a Viking warrior. Her heavy grey-green tweed suit had a long flap at the back, beneath which she'd secreted her hands as if to keep them warm. She scrutinised him as he stepped forward, declining to accept his proffered hand, but clearly expecting him to say something.

He glanced at a tray on the desk.

'Milk and two sugars, please.'

The Viking tossed the tail of her skirt into the air and turned to Quinlevan, who'd just slipped into the room.

'Piffle!'

A mighty explosion of breath emphasised the P.

'You reported him as lightweight, Q, but really—'

Quinlevan gave a slight tilt of his head as he settled into his desk chair.

'I do apologise. Hellyer, before we can take things further, we need to allay some serious concerns about your suitability for the Service. That's the reason for my senior colleague's presence.'

The warrior in the tweed suit did not introduce herself.

'Sit down. As you know, we've been looking into your past, and in the process have uncovered disturbing anomalies that need to be clarified. Now.'

The Viking glared down at him and her tone sharpened.

'Yesterday, talking to Q here, you affirmed that, as far as politics went, you had little real interest. But when you did vote, you went Liberal. So what's this then?'

She lifted a folder from the desk and thrust an eight-by-ten black-and-white glossy print in front of his nose.

'Who's that then? At a Vietnam war demonstration in Cambridge last spring. And how about this one?'

She waved another photo at him.

'An anti-nuclear weapons rally in Trafalgar Square in the autumn.'

The images were both undoubtedly of him in black donkey jacket and washed-out Levi's. In the second, he was holding the pole at one end of a CND Ban the Bomb banner.

'So are we really a little commie, then?'

The Viking was relentless.

'Not some wishy-washy liberal?'

He recalled glancing up at a first-floor window of the National Portrait Gallery as they'd entered the square, and assuming that the cameramen there were all from the press.

'So, planning world revolution, are we? Don't lie to me, sonny. You've done enough lying already.'

Her gravelly voice ground on, before he could explain or protest his innocence.

'Drugs – now, come on! You admitted you'd experimented with grass years ago, when you were young and green. But that was then, you said, and this was now.'

'I don't—'

'Liar!'

'I'm not—'

'We found traces of hash and acid in yesterday's urine test – do you really think we were born yesterday?'

His head went down.

'So we have a dope fiend here trying to join the Service, have we? Liar!'

The Viking spat the last word out, and flipped her tail again with emphasis.

'If—'

'Shut up, you streak of dirt, you dirty little fibber.'

Her perfect vowels and clear enunciation contrasted with the vituperation.

'And then there's sex. Straight, you said you were, didn't you? Girlfriends – yes, we've looked into your past flames, even talked to a couple of them. Don't ask which ones. Though, come to think of it, you can probably guess as there haven't been too many, have there? But boyfriends – you never mentioned them.'

'No.'

'Liar! What's this?'

She rammed a picture in front of his eyes – of him and Bex holding hands.

So the flashes had come from police cameras as well as strobes.

'Short memory, have we? Or a selective one? Anything more to add? We've covered politics, drugs and sex. Any other vices? Cannibalism? Serial killing? Coprophilia? Come on, spit it out. Now's the time.'

She towered above him, filling his nostrils with powerful waves of lavender cologne.

'Nothing to say for yourself?'

The Viking spun around to Quinlevan.

'Will you tell him, or shall I?'

So, after all, it was to be the magistrates' court.

The Viking continued. 'Very well, I shall. You're a liar. Admit it.'

'Yes.'

'But not a very good one – you'll have to become a much better dissimulator. As for your demos, well, it would have been concerning for us if you hadn't been on a few. Acid and hard drugs, on the other hand, are something quite different, and I express the earnest hope that your recent *trip* has shown you as much. As long as you don't have delusions about being in control of it, I suppose there's no harm in a little dope now and again. But the crucial issue is that we know about your use, so no one can blackmail you. The same goes for your sexual orientation, of course. The fact that you're bisexual could make you a powerful asset indeed, depending on where you're posted.'

She paused and cast a quick glance at Quinlevan, who nodded slightly.

'So, as far as I'm concerned, that's it, Q.'

Her gaze returned to Nick and he raised his head.

'I hope we don't meet again, because if we do it will be in circumstances far less pleasant than these.'

Delivering a final flap of her tail, the Viking marched briskly out of the room, clutching her folder of photos. Quinlevan closed the door firmly behind her and began ordering the mess of papers in front of him. Nick's state of confusion paralleled that of the desk as he watched in silent wariness.

'Well!'

He jumped at Quinlevan's bark.

'Welcome to the Intelligence Service. Don't bother with acronyms like MI5 and MI6 here – all a bit blurred nowadays, don't you know? Just think of ourselves as Intelligence – diplomacy by another name.'

A weak grin.

'Doubts, eh? With a capital D, eh? Can see you're having them. Don't worry, everyone does. Bit late now anyway, what? Just a small formality before we can proceed. Signing the Official Secrets Act.'

'Sorry, Major Quinlevan, but I don't actually have the vaguest notion of what I'm letting myself in for.'

'All a bit hush-hush and up in the clouds, don't you know? But briefly, in summary, we're sending you on a crash course in Arabic and tradecraft at MECAS. Middle East Centre for Arab Studies – FO training place at Shemlan in the Lebanon. After that you'll take up your appointment as lecturer in English Literature at an Egyptian university.'

'But why tradecraft, whatever that is? Arabic, I can understand.'

'Because in addition to your cover job you'll be undertaking certain tasks for us.'

MOD Form 134, the unimpressive piece of paper that Quinlevan handed him, had already been completed with his full name, place and date of birth.

My attention has been drawn to the provisions of the Official Secrets Act, which are set out on the reverse of this document.

Nick flipped the paper over; the page was crammed with dense single-spaced text divided into numbered paragraphs.

'No need to bother with all that small print, old boy. Now, your signature here, and mine next to it as a witness.'

He signed at once, ready to be shunted on to the next stage of his re-imagining as a secret agent.

'Excellent, Nick, if I may call you that.'

Quinlevan carefully slipped the document into a crisp new buff cardboard folder, then dropped it into his desk drawer with a flourish of his right arm.

'There, that's done so off you go. I'll be popping out to MECAS to see how you're getting on in the not-too-distant future. We'll arrange for your effects in Cambridge to be collected and stored until you need them – best not to go back there now, just in case. Your flight's not until Monday, so you'll have plenty of time to kit yourself out for the Middle East.'

***

NICK RECEIVED AN ADVANCE on salary, a hot-weather clothing supplement, a return air ticket to Beirut and a travel allowance.

He headed straight for Carnaby Street.

'Shove over, granddad. You're not the only one that wants to get a look-in, you know.'

Reflected in the boutique window, a short-haired, side-boarded, sixteen-year-old was peering over his shoulder. Perhaps Quinlevan's advice to go to Selfridges had been sound after all.

The mod's face cracked into a laugh.

'No offence, mate. Just let the dog see the rabbit.'

He moved on, jostled by gaggles of mini-skirted, bouffant-haired girls and lean-faced, sharp-suited mods trawling for the latest trend. He had secret sympathy for passing beige-macintoshed middle-aged male office workers, out of place and time. The sounds of The Modern Jazz Quartet, Muddy Waters and The Who spilled out from open shop doorways. He'd never in his life been given someone else's money to spend on clothes and was determined to make an event of it.

In the end, he seized on unisex John Stephen, where the vibe was less frenzied although the terror of choice was equally strong. His vacillation was soon sensed by a purple micro-skirted assistant, who pointed him to racks of recent arrivals.

'Here we dress the mind, love, as well as the figure.'

In the changing room, swerving to avoid a collision with the raised bum of a teenager in paisley-patterned bra and panties who was bending over to pull on a pair of Levi's, he spilled his armful of tight-waisted jackets and wide-collared shirts.

'So sorry.'

He scooped up the scatter of clothes and retreated, only to come face-to-face with the micro-skirt, chin up, arms crossed over her chest.

'Problem?'

'Ladies.'

'No. Unisex. Back in.'

Nick soon worked out that no one in the changing room had the slightest interest in checking him out. The converse, however, could not be said to be true and he was unable to resist the occasional sneak peek while he spent his way through the afternoon under the tutelage of the micro-skirt.

On his return from the fashion frenzy, he consigned his sartorial past to history, sentimentally reserving only his linen suit.

In front of the full-length mirror in the wardrobe door, he paraded in extravagant lime green flares and tie-dyed T-shirts.

***

'HEAD FORWARD AND IMAGINE you're nauseous. Now make the *xh* sound as if you were about to gob out a ball of phlegm.'

His first lesson in Arabic.

The warmth of his greeting from Amina, his tutor, had contrasted with the chilly Lebanese mountain air.

'Welcome to MECAS, Dr Hellyer. And how does it feel to be here?'

'Bit disorientated. And cold, to be truthful.'

'Don't worry. That's normal for this time of the year. And the good news is that London has just cabled – your stay is now limited to two and a half months. Your studies are going to be intensive so you won't have too much time to worry about the temperature.'

Her positive attitude and sense of humour contrasted with an underlying brusqueness.

'You'll have Arabic every morning in my group and solo tradecraft with Scottie in the afternoon. Here you'll be known as Keith. The other trainees also only use first names, which may or may not be their own.'

Amina's methods were direct, which made her lessons exciting and challenging. Just as well, as he found the phonology of Arabic hard to master and the script terrifying in its apparent absence of vowels.

Tradecraft turned out to be a crash course in espionage for dummies. Scottie, a squat middle-aged Geordie, initially did not inspire trust. But the brilliance of the man's teaching technique became clear in the title of his first session: Never Trust Anyone.

Nevertheless, he did believe that Scottie had once been a radio operator on a North Sea trawler. Nick's induction into the world of Morse Code involved painstaking hours of transcribing dots and dashes into letters and words, followed by stumbling attempts to tap out messages on a key attached to a buzzer.

'Don't think of them as dots and dashes. Think of them as sounds. Dot is *dit* and dash is *dah*. So the letter A, dot dash, is *dit-dah*, the letter B, dash dot dot dot, is *dah-dit-dit-dit*, and so on.'

More demanding close-contact sessions featured strongly. At the first, Scottie stood opposite Nick on a judo mat, chopped his right leg out from under him and fell heavily on to his chest, painfully winding him.

'Now you do the same to me.'

He caught Scottie with a sneaky kick to the left knee, but the attempted chest-fall ended with Nick face down on the mat while his teacher rolled away laughing.

A month in, he caught a brief glimpse of Major Patrick Quinlevan climbing out of the embassy Land Rover in a sweat-stained tropical suit. While the mountain air was still cool, it had clearly been unseasonably hot by the sea in Beirut. Quinlevan spent part of the morning with Amina and Scottie, and then devoted himself to Nick, clapping him enthusiastically on the shoulder.

'Good to see you, dear boy. Let's go for a walk. Nothing like a bit of fresh air, eh? And in this place' – he lowered his voice mock-conspiratorially – 'you never know who's listening.'

The two men marched away from the centre along the dusty pine-lined road leading to the village of Shemlan.

'Something to take you to task about first, young man. Expect you know what.'

Nick did. Four weeks of vacuous conversations with pseudonymous fellow students, tussles with the new language, and romps with Scottie on the mat had left him restless and lonely.

One of the canteen staff, Fathiya, had appeared amused by his flirtatious remarks in halting Arabic and the previous weekend had accepted his invitation to ice cream in the village café. Pleasantries in Arabic soon exhausted, he'd switched to

English, rashly suggesting they move on to his room in order to get to know each other better. Not his greatest idea. She'd made a complaint.

'Hellyer, you're here as a student, and students don't screw the staff. Understood?'

'Yes, Major.'

'Good. Now to business. Amina's very pleased with your progress. Apparently, you have a gift for languages. Scottie reports your Morse transcription as still a little slow. But transmission's greatly improved. Second more important than the first. Tradecraft's coming on well. Scottie will be working more on your fitness. *Fit to Fight*. Name of the training manual, you know.'

Noticing Nick puffing, the major paused.

'Exactly. Now, pay attention. Here's the plan. In March you'll take up post as Senior Lecturer in English, University of Alexandria, Egypt. British Council has already submitted your CV to the Faculty of Arts. Approval expected shortly. Teaching duties to be discussed. Understand your predecessor taught mainly final-year literature.'

'Predecessor?'

'Yes, been there for four years. Built up quite a reputation. Had to leave abruptly last autumn.'

'Why?'

Quinlevan sighed and halted, patting him on the shoulder.

'You don't need to know.'

'Will I be teaching in Arabic? Because—'

'Good God, no! It would take at least four years to bring you up to speed. Wouldn't be welcomed at all. Department prides itself that all tuition is in English. Of course, you can sprinkle your social conversation with the odd *malish* or *shukran* to be polite. And ask the way in the street. But no more than that. The Arabic is for your other role. More on that once you're in post.'

'But what is my other role? Why can't I know more now?'

'Quite simply, dear boy, way too soon. Events moving quite fast in the region. Great start made here though. Those clothes. Been noticed, I can tell you. Good you're exploring that side of yourself. As Vera remarked in my office, could come in very handy.'

'Vera?'

'Boss lady in tweed suit, remember?'

'But I'm not—'

'Main thing is to give the impression you might be.'

They marched briskly on again in silence, hands deep in pockets and heads in their own thoughts. Nick had no doubt that the university post was right up his street; as for the *other* role, he'd make up his mind when he knew what it involved.

'Talking of clothes, I'll have a word with Scottie. Time to get you used to wearing Arab costume. Need to be able to swim like a fish in the sea, you know?'

'Forgive me, Major, but I've really no idea what you're on about. And, for God's sake, why am I spending so much time learning Morse Code? Surely that's yesterday's news.'

'There, there. No need to get agitated, dear boy. Hiding in the open, don't you see?'

***

AFTER QUINLEVAN'S DEPARTURE, HE was sent out after dark, decked in a galabeya to perform small tasks, like buying sweetmeats or asking the way. While he enjoyed these challenges, he soon came to suspect that he was far from the first to be sent on this particular path. The almost too helpful villagers seemed to know his lines as well as he did.

Scottie also initiated him into the technique of sending Morse in short bursts of high-speed transmission, U-boat style.

Six weeks later, he returned to London for a blur of briefings, jabs, visa collection and packing.

***

Marseilles, 5 March 1967, 10 a.m.

THROUGH HIS CABIN PORTHOLE on the *Esperia,* Nick followed the progress of stragglers scuttling from the steep steps of the Gare Maritime across the dank mist-shrouded quay to the Alexandria-bound vessel. A joy of irresponsibility at being among strangers who could only guess as to his real identity lifted his spirits.

The first to try had been the dapper third officer in the reception line of the first-class lounge.

'But why do you need to keep my passport?'

'Because Dr Nic-ho-las, because then we can give you landing card for wherever we enter port, and you can go ashore.'

'But perhaps I won't want to.'

'But you will, believe me. Napoli, Siracusa, Beirut – these are places you will desire to see. And it is excellent you are doctor. We have ship's doctor, but always good to have more doctors.'

'No, you see, I'm an academic doctor not a medical doctor.'

'Like professor, no? Is also good. Enjoy your time with us. Here is your restaurant reservation.'

As Nick joined the assigned table for lunch a tanned, muscular man with cropped greying hair rose formally.

'This is Aisha, my wife. And our daughter, Teresa.'

Introducing himself, he half-bowed to the confident woman in a well-cut lemon trouser suit and her shining daughter.

'Mertens, Colonel Mertens. On our way back to the Lebanon – we're with the UN there. And you?'

Nick, momentarily distracted by a half-glance from Aisha, was slow to respond.

'Me? Oh, on my way to Alexandria.'

Teresa was an entrancing ten-year-old polyglot. She spoke Arabic with her Lebanese mother, Flemish to her father, Italian to the waiters, French to both her parents, and English to him.

Her mother's calm self-assurance occasionally betrayed a hint of vulnerability when her eyes hunted to and fro before responding.

***

TWO DAYS LATER, SAILING from Naples for Siracusa in Sicily, he noticed through half-open cabin doors dresses and dinner jackets being laid out, and jewellery held up for approval. Preparation for the *Pranzo di Capitano*, the captain's dinner.

When the restaurant lights dimmed, a flotilla of white-coated waiters sailed out of the kitchen, bearing salvers with ice-carved swans candle-lit from within. Nestling between raised tail feathers were silver bowls of shiny black beluga caviar.

Aisha's eyes met his as she leaned towards him.

'Wait until you get to the Lebanon, Dr Hellyer – I know you'll love our cuisine. But perhaps you've already visited.'

'No, I'm afraid I haven't.'

After dinner, coffee and liqueurs were served in the salon. As the ship's band started to play a foxtrot, Teresa stamped her foot.

'I just don't believe it. This is 1967, not 1917.'

Feeling a light tap on his upper arm, he turned to Mertens, whose index finger indicated his right leg.

'An old injury, so I don't dance. But Aisha loves to – do please invite her.'

'Delighted, of course. Just a tad afraid she'll be disappointed in me. Not the world's greatest, you know?'

Aisha's firm hand on his back as they stepped on to the tablecloth-sized dance floor quelled his fears, and he soon understood how naturally gifted she was. With the slight movement of the ship beneath their feet, she guided them through the press of other couples without making it apparent that she was leading.

As he held her closer for a waltz, her perfume wafted over him, and her body, while always held at a correct distance, on occasion brushed his.

They scarcely exchanged words but, while glancing over her shoulder at Mertens laughing with his daughter, he caught the slightest of whispers in his ear.

'Dancing isn't the only thing he's no longer able to do, I'm afraid. I can come to you when they're asleep, if you wish.'

They swirled to a halt as the band announced a break. But when an Italian disc jockey followed his self-congratulatory welcome with Pink Floyd's 'See Emily Play', Aisha slipped gently out of his arms.

'Thank you so much, Nick. Not my kind of music at all. But I know Teresa would love to dance – if you're willing.'

'Of course.'

'Later tonight.'

Teresa bounded on to the floor, but light-headed after three energetic dances, he soon returned the flushed girl to her parents.

'Must be getting too old for this kind of thing! Going to get some fresh air.'

He forced open a heavy door on to the deck and hung over the rail, assailed by Floyd-induced memories, until a flash from the shore speared his peripheral vision. Great orange arcs of tracer were raking the sky, contrasting with thick deep-red worms of glowing lava wriggling inexorably down the side of Mount Etna.

Wouldn't come to him. Woman of her class. Harmless shipboard flirtation, that was all.

But he didn't lock his cabin door before drifting off to sleep.

Then, a finger on his shoulder.

Small and delicate, it moved to her pursed lips and then to the light switch. She turned her back. The gentlest whisper.

'Come, please help me.'

Hasty, clumsy fingers complied, but then he was left stranded hanging her dress over the back of a chair.

'Hurry up, my thoughtful boy – we haven't got all night. But you must understand I'm not like this at all, or hardly ever.'

He drank in the warmth of her skin as he stroked her cheeks, kissing her eyes and then her mouth.

Afterwards, eyes closed with his head on her chest, the pounding of her heart filled his consciousness.

'But what if he wakes and you're not there?'

'I'll say I couldn't sleep and went for a night stroll on deck. Don't worry, my sweet one. I can handle this. See you at breakfast.'

With a chaste peck on the cheek, Aisha slipped out of the cabin, leaving him between sheets redolent of their lovemaking.

***

IN SIRACUSA, HE ACCOMPANIED the Mertens family on a brief visit to the remarkably intact Greek theatre. No sign of awkwardness evinced itself, and at dinner they made the usual shipboard promises of keeping in touch.

In the night Aisha came to him again.

***

THE NEXT MORNING, HAVING skipped breakfast, he sipped a cappuccino in the stern bar as the *Esperia* docked in Beirut.

Aisha gave him a firm handshake and thanked him for his company before striding confidently down the gangway with Teresa. The colonel was next.

'I'm sure you'll have a great time in Alexandria. Our paths may well cross again as I'm summoned from time to time to Cairo for regional conferences.'

With the Mertens family gone, he was assigned to a fresh table at dinner.

'Hans.'

His tall, ascetic table companion rose, offering his right hand with an ironic formal half-bow while holding his left behind his back.

'I believe we will be working together soon, or at least in the same faculty.'

'Really?'

'I suggest you don't play poker any time soon, Dr Hellyer.'

Hans gave an expansive wave of his right arm.

'Or, at least, not with me. But for sure, I know who you are. They say there are no secrets in Alexandria and that is God's truth. The full name, Hans Fussmann, Dr Hans Fussmann, or to be more correct, Dr Dr Hans Fussmann. You are teaching in the English Department, yes? After Dr Bishop? Good. I am Cherman Cultural Institute, but I give some lectures at the Faculty of Arts. So, welcome to Alexandria. You know about the city history, no?'

'Well, yes, but not in any detail, I'm afraid.'

'So you need me to inform you, and I will. Take the Pharos, the hundred-and-twenty-metre high lighthouse that stood for a thousand years. One of the Seven Wonders of the World and a triumph of Egyptian engineering – the Chermans of their day, yes?'

'Fascinating, I'm sure. But if you'll excuse me, I'm going to turn in now. Need to be fresh in the morning.'

CHAPTER 2

Alexandria, Egypt, 10 March 1967, 7 a.m.

I N THE DAWN LIGHT a smudge on the horizon became a low gap-toothed series of grey outlines gradually coming into focus as recognisable buildings. As the *Esperia* edged alongside, hawsers crashed down on to the quay and a deluge of sacks, bags and boxes followed, caught and fought over by a mob of brown-clad porters. Descending the gangway cautiously, Nick scanned the throng for a friendly face. Once on the quay, he became the immediate focus of fierce commercial competition.

'*Effendim!*'

'Taxi? Very fine.'

'You go hotel, I take you.'

'These men no good. Trust me, I help you, sir.'

A hoarse whisper in his ear. Turning, he caught the full effect of the man's well-seasoned breath, and when he lowered his bag, four pairs of hands made a grab.

A firm tap on his right shoulder from behind. An instant flashback.

He spun around and was faced with two imposing policemen in smart white uniforms. The crowd of importunate porters, having parted to let them through, maintained a ring of respectful distance.

'Dr Hellyer. Come with us.'

'Why me? What have I done?'

'Not understanding. I am Said, and this Ibrahim. British Consulate General, sir. Your baggage, please?'

Said led the way straight past the long line of dispirited passengers at customs and immigration.

'Passport, sir?'

They paused by a desk, then emerged from the cool gloom of the customs hall into the bright morning sunshine.

As the navy-blue Land Rover passed through the gates of the port and bumped along narrow dark streets, dust thrown up by its tyres swirled in shafts of sunlight and coated faded green shutters. Children, whose strikingly white teeth contrasted with shocks of black hair, screamed with delight and chased the vehicle as it slowed behind donkeys labouring under impossible-looking burdens.

Lines of sweat trickled down Nick's face and stained his shirt. He wound down his window, but instantly regretted the action as hot humid air blasted in.

Soon they were out on to a wide avenue. Men in flowing white cotton shirts tucked into grey undergarments watered roadside palms and dusty flowerbeds from long hoses.

Ten minutes later, Said turned left into a residential area.

'Bulkley, sir.'

They crossed tramlines, entering a district of low apartment blocks and houses, and pulled up outside a yellow two-storeyed villa. High-pitched cries soared over walls surrounding a large whitewashed building opposite.

'Girls' school, sir.'

As Said showed him into the parched front garden a tall grey-bearded man emerged from a ramshackle wooden dwelling by the side of the house.

'He your boab.'

'*Ahlan wa sahlan.*'

'He say welcome, sir.'

Nick was delighted to find that the hallway led into a spacious sitting room with light streaming in from small-paned, metal-framed windows on both sides.

'Fantastic.'

'This Hamid – your house servant.'

A short man in his fifties had appeared from nowhere.

'Welcome, sir.'

'Nick. Please call me Nick.'

Said patted the shorter man on the shoulder.

'Hamid look after you well. Mr Dudley, vice-consul, expecting you for lunch twelve o'clock.'

With a smile and a bow, Said gave him the vice-consul's engraved official visiting card. The two consulate staff moved towards the door and turned, half-expectantly it seemed, towards him.

Pulling a sweat-sodden Egyptian five-pound note out of his shirt breast pocket, he pressed it into the hand of Said, as the most senior of the two.

'You not understanding, sir. We British Consulate General staff.'

Said indicated his uniform and returned the note before leaving.

Arms wrapped around his shoulders, head down, he paced slowly across the room.

A polite cough.

'Sir Nick?'

Refreshed by a glass of iced water, he was taken upstairs. The double bedroom mirrored the sitting room below and could have accommodated the entirety of his Cambridge flat. Windows looked down on a barren but secluded garden.

'And where do you sleep, Hamid?'

'With my family in Sidi Gabr, sir.'

Thank God they were in Sidi Gabr, wherever that was, and not in situ.

He set off for the vice-consul's apartment, chin up and head held high, following Hamid's directions. A prolonged horn blast from a brightly painted truck laden with building materials propelled him into rough vegetation by the side of the road, where he narrowly avoided a muddy slither into a foul-smelling ditch.

Curious stares followed him as he trudged on, gradually becoming aware that he'd lost his way. He paused by two old men sitting on upturned wooden boxes in front of a workshop emitting metallic banging noises and blue flashes.

Just as he was about to approach them, a small beige Nasr car pulled up a little further along the street.

He trotted quickly over and leant into the driver's open window.

'*Min fadlak, fayn il unsuliyya ingileezi?*'

The thickset stubbled driver in dark glasses wound up the window and raised his copy of that day's *Al Ahram*. When Nick tapped again the driver peered at him over the top of the newspaper before driving off.

Puzzled but undeterred, he returned to the old men and repeated the question. One pointed ahead with his stick.

'British Consulate, *alatool*, straight on.'

Before he could set off, a group of boys aged no more than ten surrounded him. A bold one tugged at his right sleeve, rubbing his grubby thumb over his fingertips and then holding his hand out, palm up.

'*Baksheesh, effendim.*'

He smiled and dropped a few piastres into the boy's palm but the others immediately thrust out their hands. Flinging his remaining coins into the dust, he fled down a side street.

His headlong flight brought him out on to a wider avenue, which he thought he recognised from the morning. He was marching along as fast as he could when a yellow and black pre-war Morris taxi hooted and pulled in beside him.

'Where you going, sir?'

'British Consulate General.'

'In Rouchdy, sir, I am knowing.'

The elderly vehicle did a U-turn, retracing most of his route until it took a sharp right and roared up Kafr Abdou. Three quarters of the way up the hill, momentum lost, it juddered to a clattering halt. The driver jumped out with an apologetic wave of the hand, so Nick paid him off and walked the rest of the way.

In a small park, children raced on bicycles with spokes interlaced with brightly coloured toilet paper. The British Consulate General, a wedding-cake-style two-storey white building, lay to his left. To his right, the Dafrawi Building, where vice-consul Colin Dudley lived, rose above surrounding trees. Outside it a now-familiar beige Nasr stood, the driver deep in his study of the newspaper.

The handsome boab at the top of the shining marble steps swung open the double glass doors and ushered him into a wood-panelled lift.

Dudley, who opened the sixth-floor apartment door after the first ring, combined sharp eyes with an open manner, and was more youthful than Nick had expected.

'Ah, Dr Hellyer. I was beginning to wonder …'

The vice-consul waved him into an extensive lounge. Long picture windows along one side offered spectacular views down to the Mediterranean.

'Drink?'

Dudley vanished.

As Nick was taking in the highly polished parquet floor overlaid with intricately patterned Turkish rugs, Dudley reappeared bearing a polished brass tray with glasses and two golden cans of Whitbread Pale Ale.

'I'm Col. Cheers.'

'Nick.'

'Get the beer from the embassy shop in Cairo. Perk of the job. 'Fraid you're not able to, but the local brew's good enough. Trouble finding this place?'

His account mentioned the man with the stick and the uncommunicative driver of the beige Nasr.

'Yes, the old guy you met was right in a way. Consulate General used to be in the centre. As for the car, you're new here so you're bound to be of interest. Gyppos paranoid about espionage – think every westerner's a spy.'

'What's been your experience, then?'

Col put his finger to his lips and cupped one ear with the palm of his hand.

'Can I ask your advice about something else then? You see, I've got this boab at my place, and then there's Hamid, the house servant. What do I need them for? You don't appear to have any servants here.'

'Ah, yes. Well, all not as it seems. Actually, sent mine home early today. Grace is in the UK at the mo, getting the boys back to boarding school. Only six and seven, so a bit of a wrench. Yasmeen's our maid, and a girl helps her with the cleaning. Important, you know, to understand that all this gives people work.'

'My boab. What exactly does he do?'

'Looks after the outside of the house, a bit of gardening I expect, security, keeps an eye on comings and goings. Very useful.'

'But I really don't need a full-time servant like Hamid – I can look after myself.'

'So you say. But I'd give it a little while, if I were you. Now, let's buzz and get something to eat. Also easier to talk freely in the open air, if you get my drift.'

Outside the Dafrawi Building, behind the Nasr, Said waited at the wheel of a white Ford Zodiac with diplomatic number plates. Their route took them past anonymous apartment blocks with canopy-shaded balconies, juxtaposed with decaying mansions and vacant plots. On the other side of the tarmac, the Mediterranean glistened and wavelets rolled on to occasional empty beaches.

'Won't spot a vacant piece of sand in summer – littered with wealthy Cairenes. Got a little seaside place ourselves out of town at Agami. Peaceful all year round there. You must come out.'

The car swept along the Corniche all the way to Fort Quait Bey, and they walked the last few metres down the quay to the blue-and-white-painted Greek Club.

Seated upstairs on the terrace, looking out over the Eastern Harbour, Nick recalled his final instructions. 'Just build your cover, an ambivalent bisexual image. There've been plenty like that before you, so that's what they'll expect.'

Col raised his glass of ice-cold Stella.

'Welcome to the United Arab Republic, Nick. Fairly safe to talk here. Best to assume that both the Consulate General and my flat are bugged, as are the phones. International calls have to be booked in advance. Mind you, use any language other than English, French or Arabic and they'll cut you off – not that yours truly speaks more than one of those. Okay?'

Nick nodded.

'Look, let's get business out of the way before we eat. Come into the office in a day or two – no secure facilities there, mark you. Your equipment has arrived. You'll know what that's for and I'll set it up. No personal diplomatic bag facilities for you, I'm afraid. I can take stuff to the embassy once a week for onward transmission to your people. And you'll need to get yourself down there anyway to make your number with the cultural attaché.'

'But surely the Egyptians will suspect something if I'm in and out of the consulate all the time.'

'Naturally. But, as you've found out, they already suspect you. Would be much more suspicious if we had no contact at all. Now, tomorrow you've got an appointment at the Faculty of Arts with Professor Naguib, Head of the English Department.'

'I look forward to meeting him.'

'Her. Plenty of women in posts of responsibility – something Nasser isn't always given credit for.'

'Bit of a cheek, I know, but can I ask how you ended up here?'

'Well, I wasn't born to this lark. After university – first time for someone in my family – started at the FO in London, made second vice-consul, Athens, then this place. I keep my eyes and ears open, deal with Commonwealth War Graves at El Alamein, and everything else from virtually non-existent shipping to elderly British passport-holders. Love it myself, but not so much fun for Grace.'

'I was wondering about my predecessor, and why he left so precipitately.'

'Ah, yes, well there's a thing. Not for me that one, I'm afraid. Did I say your appointment tomorrow was at nine? Get in touch after that, and pop in to meet Winks, my lord and master.'

Col left for a meeting at the consulate and Nick turned his attention to the fishing boats puffing their way cautiously through the crowded harbour. Sunlight danced on their cockpits and bounced off the windows ringing the bay, turning it into an amphitheatre of mirrors.

Nick hopped on a battered 1920s tram and headed for the open top deck. As the rock-and-roll ride took him past the Al Shatby stop for the university, he resolved to sort things out with Hamid.

On his arrival, the servant politely asked what he'd like for supper. Still replete from lunch, Nick unthinkingly followed him into the kitchen, only to contemplate empty pantry shelves and the equally barren American-style refrigerator containing only a jug of boiled water.

Probably a good idea to postpone that discussion.

CHAPTER 3

NICK WAS JOLTED AWAKE by high-pitched shrieks from the playground. Sunshine pierced the narrow wooden shutters and striped his bedspread.

He lurched to the bathroom. Unfamiliar with the shower controls, he doused himself with alternating sprays of scalding hot and cool water.

A rummage through drawers containing the results of Hamid's random unpacking produced a bottle-green jacket and fuchsia-pink flares. Not exactly formal, but the best he could do. Unable to do justice to the breakfast offering of mango, rolls and coffee, he tore out of the house towards the tram stop.

Most of the passengers on the top deck were men deep in conversation, the newspaper or the pleasure of a morning cigarette. However, a few made no secret of their curiosity. He ignored them, faking a deep interest in the irregular lines of raw bricks on jerry-built apartment blocks.

When he alighted a muted but distinct chorus of '*Ya howell!*'– 'You faggot!' – brought to mind Amina's colloquial language classes.

El-Guish Road led to the Faculty of Arts, a pleasantly weathered ochre building of six storeys constructed in the

1950s. Directed to the English Department, he wandered past chattering students and down an echoing, tiled corridor to a flight of stairs.

The professor's office was dominated by a huge desk fortified with a barrier of files, behind which a severe-looking middle-aged woman sat typing vigorously.

'Excuse me, Professor Naguib. I do apologise for interrupting you.'

The hammering ceased. The woman removed her large black-framed glasses and stared up at him as if he were some unwelcome exotic creature.

'Professor Naguib is occupied at the moment. My role is that of department secretary, so please tell me your business. If you have time at your disposal, the professor may conceivably be able to fit you in later.'

Her tone was as cold and dismissive as her English was perfect.

'Dr Nicholas Hellyer. I was given to believe the professor was expecting me at nine o'clock this morning.'

She took in him in again, now more thoughtfully.

'We were expecting someone rather more ... but do please take a seat.'

The secretary disappeared through a connecting door to the professor's office.

A minute later, a short, stocky woman stormed in. Blonde-streaked wiry dark hair, thick eyebrows, and the bold slash of lipstick on her lips gave her an almost piratical appearance. Her broad smile revealed a flash of gold.

'Dr Hellyer! You surprised us! You're early. Not a trait we ever had cause to associate with your predecessor, I must say. Come in, come in. We're so pleased to see you. So now – would you like tea or coffee? I know – we can bring both and you can decide. Rachida, two teas and two coffees, please.'

The professor took his arm, leading him through into her office and showing him to a low dark-wood coffee table and two heavy leather armchairs.

'Now, you must tell me all about yourself.'

But before he could, she continued rapidly.

'It's been a nightmare since Bishop abandoned us so abruptly. He'd been with us for four years and we'd become used to him and his, shall I say, slightly unorthodox ways. He'd only teach certain courses, so it was extremely difficult for us to cover for him last term. But now you're here everything will be all right. You're our saviour, Dr Hellyer.'

'Can I ask why my predecessor left?'

The professor left the question hanging in the air as a thin elderly man entered, dwarfed by a hanging brass tray on which stood two tall glasses of clear dark tea with swirls of leaves at the bottom, two heavier glasses of water, two long-handled copper coffee pots and two cups.

Her seeming reluctance to answer left him unsure as to how he should respond, so he swallowed the coffee in one go, leaving himself with a mouthful of grounds. After taking a gulp of water, he reached for a glass of tea.

'Excellent, Dr Hellyer. I can see you're going to fit in with us just fine. Now, about your teaching. Bishop offered three courses, each two hours a week: Elizabethan and Jacobean drama, metaphysical poetry and the Victorian novel. How do you feel about taking those on?'

Silent thanks to Bishop. The cornerstones of the Cambridge Tripos, which he knew so well.

'In this folder you'll find details of what we were able to cover last term – not as much as we'd have wished, I'm afraid. And it also contains Dr Bishop's comprehensive course outlines. Now, I'm all ears. You were going to tell me about yourself.'

As he briefly sketched his academic career, he puzzled over why she appeared not to recall the CV the British Council had reportedly submitted.

'Well, we must have long chats about Cambridge when there's time – my husband trained as a doctor there many moons ago. Rachida will fill you in on lecture times and dates, and introduce you to Richard. He's the other foreign lecturer in the department.'

She stood up, holding out her hand: the interview was clearly at an end and Nick left the office.

The secretary pulled a sheet from her typewriter.

'Here's your timetable, Dr Hellyer. You have two hours a day – mornings, nine to eleven, Monday, Tuesday, Wednesday – and two hours' advanced English conversation on Tuesday afternoon. All with the final year. You'll also note that Bishop negotiated himself a particularly fine deal.'

Rachida sniffed and glanced up at the ceiling in some silent appeal.

'If you'd be so kind as to wait here, Richard will be by shortly to collect you.'

Nick reclined awkwardly on a low sofa with his knees high in the air. Bishop had clearly had only one priority: himself.

So he was free all day Thursday, Friday, Saturday and Sunday.

A thin, earnest-looking man peered around the door and introduced himself.

They moved to the empty staffroom, its long Formica-topped table littered with abandoned cups and glasses. Curtains permeated with the stench of stale tobacco flapped next to half-open windows.

'We don't tend to use this very much, I'm afraid. Colleagues mainly come in to the department, do their classes, and go home again. Private lessons often take up a lot of time – people need to make ends meet, you see.'

'So money's tight?'

'You can say that again. Might as well mention that Marwa and I had hoped that when Bishop vanished I'd take over his role. We're expecting our second child soon.'

'Sorry about the way things worked out for you.'

'Not your fault, Nick. Now, I'm supposed to bring you up to speed on how things function in the department. So let's deal with that as we walk, and I can show you around a bit at the same time.'

In the event, Richard was more eager to please as a guide to the city than to university bureaucracy.

'Bar in the Cecil isn't really what it's cracked up to be, but you've got to try it once for the wartime connection. Down that way towards Ras-El-Tin, you'll find the Spitfire – bit of an international seamen's hangout. Up here's the Roman amphitheatre they call Kom Al-Dikka, the pile of rubble. And, just along here on Safeya Zaghloul is the Elite, where we can take a break.'

Richard took him into a light and airy one-storey café sticking out on to the pavement.

'Hope you don't mind. Bit of a rabbit out of a hat, I know, but bear with me. I knew I'd have to show you around, so I asked a few people from the department to join us here.

You see, Bishop used to direct plays – *Look Back in Anger*, that kind of stuff.'

'So you—'

'Thing is that last autumn we started rehearsing a play by an Egyptian friend of Bishop's – a black comedy. He'd reserved one of the more demanding roles for himself. Truth be told, we've been scratching around for a suitable replacement ever since he left.'

Before Nick could respond, the twin doors of the Elite banged wide open. A barrel-chested man with a broad grin burst in, dragging behind him two not-too-reluctant young women.

'Lucky and his wife, Sohail. Samira's her sister.'

The doors swung again to herald a confident slight woman, all in black, and a young man with floppy hair.

'Leila's also in the cast and Samy's helping us with props and lights.'

Animated overlapping conversations broke out around Nick, not about the drama project at all, but about art – some of the paintings on display came in for severe criticism – literature, life in Alexandria, and departmental gossip. Everything except politics and what he was doing there. Which they must have known.

Richard ordered coffees and ice creams for all, taking his and Nick's to a side table.

'A bit sudden I know, but we want to start rehearsals again. However, we've nowhere to go. We used to use Bishop's place, your house now.'

'Well, I suppose so, yes. If it helps. But I've absolutely no acting experience.'

'Fantastic – we all hoped you would. And let me be the judge of your suitability.'

After the group had broken up with hugs and embraces, Nick walked back alone to Ramleh Station, playing at being a spy. He feigned interest in reflective shop windows, recalling faces of the vibrant group of young people he'd just met. He freeze-framed each one. Trustworthy? Of use? Lightweight?

***

THE WEEKS THAT FOLLOWED assumed a pleasing rhythm. Saturdays and Sundays he spent preparing lectures for the twenty quick-witted, largely bilingual, final-year students. And he did his three days of teaching and hosted the Thursday-evening rehearsals. Friday was the Egyptian weekend, dedicated to solo walks around the city, armed with E.M. Forster's guidebook.

He'd met Winks, the consul general, who clearly believed he'd been destined for better things.

A late-night tour of the bars with Richard, including the Spitfire, had celebrated the arrival of his and Marwa's baby boy.

He'd been to the professor's house and had tea with her and her husband, who was in the Faculty of Medicine, and accompanied Col to the Goethe Institut for a reception in honour of a visiting string quartet. When he expressed surprise at Hans's absence, Col had put him straight.

'Fussmann is the DDR Cultural Centre Director, and therefore persona non grata here in the West German one. Anyway, how did you meet him?'

***

'THIS IS MAMDOUH — only has a few words of English.'

Introduced at the first rehearsal, the playwright bore a disturbing resemblance to Jimi Hendrix, with a head of wiry hair and strong cheekbones. Nick learned that he was to play a bumbling police inspector investigating a series of murders.

Lucky turned out to be a naturally gifted comic, Sohail and Samira sharply intelligent and outspoken, Leila more self-contained. The group arrived and left together, except for Samy, who usually stayed behind to help clear up, assistance for which Nick was grateful.

After the third rehearsal, Samy complained of dizziness and a blinding headache, so Nick offered to put him up for the night.

'Thank you, that's kind. You're very sweet, and so was Bishop.'

His predecessor was always referred to as if he were a chess piece.

'Bishop was wonderful to me. He was my dear friend, you understand – we used to read Cavafy together.' Samy's face darkened. 'Then that Mamdouh came along and all Bishop could see was him.'

'Now, now, Samy. Let's have a nice cup of tea.'

As they sat side by side on the sofa, Samy poured out his heart. Nick extended an awkward arm around his shoulder and patted his back.

'There, there.'

'Can I lie down with you?'

Nick smiled warmly but shook his head.

'Let me show you where the spare bedroom is – you need to rest. I'll see you in the morning.'

Mercifully, as it was Friday, Hamid was not there to greet them over the breakfast table. Samy seemed fully recovered as they drank tea in the garden in the warm late-March sunshine.

'Did you really do those drawings, Nick?'

He'd hung some of his sketches in the sitting room.

'Well, yes.'

'Oh, will you draw me? Please?'

Nick retrieved his sketchbook and pencils. When he returned, Samy was half-sitting, half-lying on the large uphol-stered garden swing and had taken off his shirt.

'Right, keep still – this could take a little while.'

He focused on his drawing and, to his surprise, found Samy to be a good subject who held the pose well. Half an hour later, his concentration was interrupted by a whoop from Col peering around the corner of the house at Nick and a half-naked, reclining young man.

'Morning, squire! Let myself in. Just dropped by with this – came in yesterday's bag.'

Col held out an official-looking brown envelope and took in the scene with a foxy grin.

'Won't stay now – can see you've got your hands full. Did I say Grace was back? Wondered if you'd like to come over this evening for a bite to eat. Make up a foursome at bridge. Shall we say seven?'

'Delighted.'

Nick clutched his sketchbook tightly to his chest.

'Righty ho. See you then. Bye. And bye to …' Col gazed stagily at the model, his hand horizontal over his eyebrows.

'Samy.'

'Bye, Samy. Hope to meet you again sometime soon.'

Nick was philosophical – Col would doubtless report back that he was following Bishop's example.

After Samy had departed with the completed sketch, Nick poured himself a slug of Egyptian gin and the splendidly named *tonk wotar* before reading the Diplomatic Wireless Service message Col had delivered.

> *Quinlevan arriving Wednesday 20. Meeting at Embassy Thursday 21, 11.00.*

***

PROMPT AT SEVEN, IN high-waisted tangerine flares and concerned that he might have overdone the Old Spice deodorant, he presented himself at the Dudleys. The door was flung open by a vision of flying ash-blonde hair and flashing green eyes.

'Come in, sweetie. You must be Nick. I've heard so much about you.'

Mrs Grace Dudley took his arm and virtually marched him into the lounge, where Col was serving drinks to the consul general and Mrs Winks.

'Here he is, my new man in Alexandria!'

Still in shock, he was introduced to Mrs Edith Winks, whose clothes taste had been moulded forever by post-war austerity. The consul general stood up.

'Capital. Glad you could make it at such short notice. Can't stay after dinner, I'm afraid. Bit of a shout going on at the office.' Winks put his index finger to his lips. 'Col tells me you'll be Edith's bridge partner.'

Grace immediately summoned them into the dining room for a bland three-course dinner, prepared and served by Yasmeen.

Nick fended off polite enquiries about his background from the Winkses while trying to come to terms with a glaring contradiction. He could not reconcile Grace's vivacity and vibrancy with this dull, Surrey on a plate, English middle-class life transported to Egypt.

'Know Friday's usually Yasmeen's day off. But have only just got back so sure she didn't mind working tonight.' She held up her glass for Col to refill. 'Expect she's had her hands full looking after you, hasn't she, dear? Not in that way, of course. Wouldn't dare, would you?' She cackled, fixing her husband with a mock steely eye.

Winks rapidly steered matters back to safer ground with an enquiry about their children's schooling.

Nick ate his food largely in silence, with little to contribute to the conversation.

After Winks had left self-importantly, Col informed him in a stage whisper that nothing earth-shattering was calling the consul general away; he just couldn't stand bridge.

Nick sat opposite Edith, trying to respond positively to her excessively timid bidding. Grace was to his right.

Col and Grace were a well-matched team, with her seemingly reckless bids often going home through her husband's skilful play. Meanwhile, he and Edith were losing slowly but inexorably.

When it was Grace's turn to deal again, a card dropped to the floor.

'Whoops! I'll get it.'

'Allow me.'

As he and Grace ducked simultaneously under the heavy tablecloth, their eyes met and hands brushed as they competed to grab the fallen card. She held his hand briefly before taking the card and backing out. A crash and a cry followed as she collided with the table.

'Whoops again!'

She emerged with a rueful grin, rubbing her head as Nick took his seat.

After the game had drawn to its inevitable conclusion, Col offered to escort Mrs Winks back to the Residence. Nick volunteered to help tidy up, depositing a tray of cups and glasses on the kitchen table.

'Where do you want them?'

'Where do I want what?' Grace purred, and launched herself at him.

Sharp nails dug into his shoulders. Initial shock and fear of the consequences evaporated as his exploring hands found that nowhere was forbidden, everything permitted.

Releasing her grip and sliding down his chest, she faced him, panting.

'Listen. Plan. He'll be back in a minute. Tomorrow, Agami. I'll take you there. He has to work but knows I want to go. Thinks I'm safe with you as you're a poof. Officially. Now get back into the lounge.'

Leafing through a colour brochure extolling the progress of the British tractor industry, he looked up nervously when Col returned.

'Many thanks, Nick – know Edith isn't the greatest partner. Why not stay and keep us company in a brandy?'

'And he's offered to keep *me* company tomorrow in Agami.'

'Most grateful, squire. For my sins, got a visiting delegation. Course, generally Alex is safe as houses – don't you worry. But a European woman on her own? Would feel better knowing someone was with her.'

'What bollocks, darling.' Grace placed a hand on her husband's arm. 'You know very well that I can look after myself.'

She accompanied Nick out to the lift.

'Come up at ten and don't forget your swimming things. Temperature's still lowish, but could get a lot steamier.'

He took two wrong turnings on the way home.

***

THINGS WERE ALREADY HEATING up the next morning as he climbed Kafr Abdou, prepared for a day at the beach, bring what it might.

Perched with crossed legs on the bonnet of a yellow Vauxhall Viva outside the Dafrawi Building, hair captured inside a white silk headscarf, dazzling eyes hidden behind red-framed sunglasses, figure concealed beneath a long-sleeved high-collared shirt, Grace waited for him.

'Well, how is my man in Alexandria today?'

As she negotiated the traffic with evident pleasure, a more confiding tone of voice revealed a different persona from the previous night.

'Fine. Looking forward to getting to know you and this place better.'

'One is easier than the other.'

Her hand fell casually on his left knee as he took in the passing city. The buildings appeared sometimes graceful, often decrepit, occasionally garish, but the juxtaposition of this seemingly endless curve of tarmac with the shining sea was remarkable.

'You love it, don't you? Already. I can see it.'

In telling vignettes, she described the concerts and exhibitions promoted by the competing cultural institutes and attended by fading former Alexandrian society, governorate officials and their wives, and a few ageing expatriates, as well as the university staff and students who were the main targets of it all.

'You dress well. I noticed that. Could introduce you to Hanneaux, best department store in town. They're wizards at copying clothes in the finest Egyptian cotton – all for peanuts. I can show you what's what, if you like.'

'Yes, please. I'm sure you can.'

Passing Fort Quait Bey they turned left to follow the coastline. In a poorer district, with lower buildings crammed together, she pulled over opposite a fish-market.

'Came down here at five in the morning once – friend took me. See that wall with the torn posters? By it was a line of women, all in long black garments with bright-coloured headscarves, queuing. Feverish excitement when heavy baskets carried out of the port.

In them, turtles. They cut their throats, drain the blood, and the women buy it. And drink, then and there. Makes them fat, which is highly prized. A very sensual place, you know, Alexandria. Can't you feel it in the air? Passion?'

He looked across at the market. No signs of sex there. Tattered light-brown tarpaulins on wooden rafters part-shielded some of the fish sellers, whose neat arrangements of red and grey mullet pointed up to the sky. The smell of the catch almost, but not quite, drowned out the fumes from the buses, cars, taxis, trucks and motorbikes crawling past, only a couple of metres from the careful displays.

'Enough?'

She rejoined the line of traffic slowly bumping its way over increasingly potholed roads in the district of Mex.

'Lake Mariout on the left. Been there since ancient times. Fishermen in punts, mud, marshes. Pretty stinky, actually. City's always been caught between the lake and the sea.'

They'd left an area of refineries and now drove faster on a narrower road.

'Carry on up here, you get to El Alamein. Then Mersa Matruh, then Libya. Nothing to stop you. Indeed, nothing to stop Rommel in 1942 coming the other way, either. Apart from Montgomery, that is. And now the Germans are back again. Better believe it.'

She glanced at him over her sunglasses.

Soon she hung an abrupt right down what became a grassy sand-covered track and halted outside a two-storey flat-roofed concrete beach house. He glimpsed a flash of shining sea as he swung his sandaled feet out of the car on to the surprisingly warm sand.

She handed him a picnic hamper and opened up the house.

'Last one in the sea's a sissy.'

She dropped her jeans, threw off her shirt and sprang off in her bikini.

On the beach, to the right, a promontory was capped with an old fort; to the left, brilliant white sand; and ahead, turquoise water.

Grace raced in, splashing out a long way before it became deep enough to swim properly. Small groups of leathery elderly men in sunglasses and capacious swimming shorts, large enough to carry cigarettes and matches, stood with water up to their lower thighs, recounting long-forgotten disputes and triumphs.

Nick swam far out on his own, then returned to float companionably beside her.

On their return to the beach house, she opened the hamper, delegated the corkscrew to him and laid out the picnic food. They lunched downstairs, wrapped in thick white cotton dressing gowns. He was surprisingly hungry, and it was only after they'd finished that he realised he'd hardly said a word throughout yet another meal.

'Like your silence. Come upstairs.'

He lay naked on the bed, wondering which of the several Graces was about to come to him. As she emerged from the bathroom, his eyes were drawn to her sharp pointed breasts, which ended in smooth pink cones.

'Know what you're looking at. No nipples. Don't worry. Super, super sensitive.'

She ran her hands over his chest and down his body, caressing him almost everywhere, but not there where he so wanted her attention.

'Trust me and lie still now.'

She slid the glass doors of the balcony to a close, then surveyed him from the foot of the bed for an excruciatingly long moment before lightly scratching her way up his legs and body. She rose on to her knees and moved forward until she was kneeling immediately over him. He squinted up, past her belly, to her eyes framed in the sunlight by her ash-blonde hair.

'Now, my Nick.'

She lowered herself on to his face.

'Lick.'

***

GRACE SLID OFF NICK and lay silently with her head on his shoulder for a few minutes, entwining her forefinger in his chest hairs before strolling naked downstairs and returning with two glasses of cool white wine. She gave him a sip from one and drained the other as she stood over him by the side of the bed.

'Gracie! *Liebchen*. Gracie!'

A loud male voice.

'It's your Hansie. Let me in.'

'Fuck! I'll get rid of him.'

She slipped on her dressing gown, took a slurp from his glass and trotted downstairs.

'Saw your car, my Gracie – so I guessed you were here.'

'Yes, love, on my lonely ownsome. But do come in for a moment anyway. How are you? It's great to see you again, you sexy man, you.'

So it was the German from the *Esperia*.

Grace had reverted to the loud flirty role of the evening before.

'Fine. It's quite a long time, no?'

'Been in the UK, you know – just got back. And how have you filled in your time while I've been away, Hansie dear? With your lovely wifey?'

'So sorry, but I wonder, can I use your bathroom, please?'

Hans clearly knew his way around because he started up the stairs at speed without waiting for a reply. Nick heard the shoes on the concrete steps, closed his eyes and awaited the inevitable humiliation.

'Hansie, come back, you silly man.'

Nick found her tone far too relaxed.

'Toilet's still not working. If you must piss, go out the back and do it against the wall. That's an advantage you men have.'

She gave a dirty chuckle. Footsteps retreated, a door opened and closed, and a minute later the German returned.

'Look Hans, sweetie, it's like this. Not feeling too great at the moment, you understand. Came out here to get a bit of peace.'

'So I see. When can we meet then?' Hans had morphed into a small boy denied a treat. 'Are you coming to the exhibition on Tuesday? Perhaps I could lend my colleague's flat?'

'Yes, that might work. Let's see.'

'Okay. So I'll go then.'

'Bye, sweetie.'

The front door closed and she came up with the bottle of wine.

'Sorry about that.'

'Friend of yours?'

'Sort of. Attached himself to me one night after a particularly awful diplomatic dinner. Now, as you can see …' She shrugged. 'That was then, but this is now.'

'Why me?'

She put the wine down and cuddled up to him with her head on his shoulders, stroking his face.

'Something in you called to me. Know you're not what you pretend to be – and, for the record, neither am I. Col and I have been together a long time. Since university, actually. But I've always thought he got me cheaply.'

Gently she kissed the centre of his forehead.

He so much wanted to believe her – a woman unlike any he'd ever known. Yet he shivered and the hairs on his arm stood up.

'With the first child coming when I was twenty, I was lucky to get a decent degree. No, he's got the career, for what it's worth, and I'm the one who's in tow.'

Nothing was more convincing than when you want to be convinced.

'Did you know that as a diplomatic wife I'm not allowed to work in Egypt?'

For whom?

'Now, that's enough of me. Let's see what we can do with this poor stricken thing.'

She threw off her gown and turned her full attention to Nick, who, overwhelmed, responded almost at once.

'What if someone else hears us?'

'To the ordinary Egyptian, we're foreigners whose entire behaviour is inexplicable. Anyway, the secret police have probably recorded the whole event. Only joking, of course.'

'You blow me away, Grace. You move me, you know that? And we've hardly spoken. But what about Col and you, and work?'

'Leave Col to me. Anyway, you're officially gay, so a suitable escort. Tomorrow afternoon I'll introduce you to Hanneaux. Have the clothes you want copied ready.'

They drove back in close amicable silence through the fading afternoon light and she dropped him off at his gate.

***

AT TWO O'CLOCK THE next day, Grace pulled up outside with Col beside her.

'Afternoon, sunshine. Thought I'd tag along and get a few more shirts made up.'

The courteous, knowledgeable French-speaking staff of Hanneaux had been starved of the latest fashions and fell upon the clothes Nick had brought in. Under Grace's guidance, he ordered copies of three shirts and three pairs of flares in a range of colours.

Grace was in flirtatious mode, commenting loudly to Col on how assiduous the young tailor was in measuring Nick's inside leg.

'Be that as it may, my love, he ought to know that copies of his precious clothes will soon be on display in the shop window.'

Afterwards, they drove the length of the Corniche to Montazah and ex-King Farouk's palace for a walk among the pine trees overlooking the crashing waves.

The three days' teaching passed in satisfactory fashion, with Nick relishing the exchanges with his students, gradually getting to grips with their sense of humour. When he glossed 'nightsoil' as 'human faeces collected from households by a cart', an earnest bespectacled woman in the front spoke up.

'Same here, sir. Collected from poor districts and used as fertiliser, sir. Excellent for strawberries. Have you tried?'

'Yes, I have.'

The student suppressed a smile with a hand to her mouth. He didn't have strawberries again for a while, though.

***

ON WEDNESDAY AFTERNOON, THE silver Hungarian-made train pulled smoothly into Sidi Gabr Station and he boarded his air-conditioned first-class carriage and found the seat reservation for which Hamid had queued the day before.

The smoked glass of his window was a movie screen on which he could observe the life of the Delta as it slipped by: the *fellaheen* working the rich soil as they had done for thousands of years, and the donkeys plodding endlessly in circles, bound to wheels of irrigation buckets. To the men in the towns who climbed through holes in the high white-washed mud-brick walls beside the track, hoiked up their galabeyas, squatted and shat on the ground, his gaze could have been that of an alien.

He arrived at the Nile Hotel in fading light, the pinkish tinge of the sky sharpening the outlines of ragged black clouds. Later, on Col's recommendation, he walked along the honking, malodorous Nile embankment past the Zamalek Bridge on which fodder-laden carts held up hopelessly overfilled buses, and on to the air-conditioned sanctuary of the Hilton.

'No, sorry, sir.'

The Nubian headwaiter by the tall desk at the entrance to the first-floor buffet restaurant, with its huge windows overlooking the river, was adamant.

'But there are plenty of empty tables – they can't all be reserved.'

'No tie, no jacket, no entry, sir.'

He shrugged and turned to walk away.

'Sir, sir. This way, please.'

The headwaiter led him to a cloakroom in a side corridor. He switched on lights to reveal rack upon rack of jackets and ties for Nick to choose from.

A country where everything was impossible and possible at the same time. *Mish mumkin* and *mumkin*.

***

THE NEXT MORNING, HE sipped coffee on his balcony, the compound of the embassy laid out beneath him. The main buildings were of an age with the Alexandria Consulate General. To his left was the Residence with lawns, swimming pool and a tennis court where some keen young things were enthusiastically hitting balls into the net.

He presented himself at the modern administration block at ten o'clock and the security guard buzzed him through for his appointment with Mr Tomkins.

The cultural attaché, who affected a lumberjack shirt and high-heeled yellow leather cowboy boots, ran his fingers through long slicked-back mousy blond hair.

'So you're the new lecturer in Alexandria. Capital! Heard from the consul general that you're settling in well. Also had a nice letter from your Professor Nag.'

'Naguib.'

'Ah, yes, that's the chap.'

'Lady.'

'Wish you wouldn't keep interrupting, Hell.'

'Hellyer.'

'There, you're doing it again. So why do you want to see me?'

'Just a courtesy call, sir.'

A snort and a dismissive wave of the arm.

'Plenty of better-qualified people than you applied for the post, don't you know? But it was *suggested* by your shadowy friends that you were the ideal candidate, so I have to tolerate you.'

With this, Tomkins swung his booted feet up on to his desk and resumed his scrutiny of *The Times Literary Supplement*.

Nick's appointment with Quinlevan was not for another hour, so he stepped outside into the sunshine of the courtyard.

'Well, hello. This is a good surprise!'

Colonel Mertens in full uniform.

'Aisha will certainly be pleased I saw you. Must meet up when I get down to Alex one of these days. Sorry I can't stop to chat – late for a conference of regional defence attachés. So much happening just now, you understand.'

At eleven, Nick presented himself to the security guard at the desk and was asked again for his passport. A button was pressed and two blue-uniformed men escorted him into a side room. Seated between them, his eyes glazed over at fading watercolours of London and his head dropped.

Half an hour later, a flushed, harassed-looking young woman poked her head around the door.

'Oh, there you are. Our visitor from London's in a meeting, I'm afraid. He does know you're here. So sorry about all of this.' She gestured to the uniformed men either side of him. 'Heightened security just now. Much easier, I'd suggest, if you go back to your hotel. Your contact will join you as soon as he's free.'

***

ON THE TOP-FLOOR TERRACE of the Nile Hotel Nick sulkily slumped into a cracked red plastic chair, the back of which immediately gave way, depositing him on the tiles.

What a bastard that Tomkins had been. No reason on earth, apart from his poppycock self-esteem, to treat him like that. And Quinlevan could have arranged to meet him at the hotel from the start.

A waiter brought an ice-cold Stella and groundnuts. He took his drink over to the railings and idly watched ragged black vultures circling over the British embassy. The minarets of the Al-Azhar Mosque were visible over his right shoulder.

'Well, dear boy, many congratulations. Everyone speaks very highly of you and you appear to have charmed both the university and the consulate.'

While he welcomed the sound of Quinlevan's ever positive voice, he wasn't convinced of the truth of his words.

'Don't think I charmed Tomkins today. Oh, and is it safe to talk here?'

'Good question. You're a quick learner.'

Praise – but the accompanying smile was more than slightly patronising.

'Yes, unless they've put a directional microphone up one of the vultures' arses. And I wouldn't want to be the brave person who tried to do that.'

Quinlevan. Treating him almost as an equal, but still holding back his trump card. Power.

'Ironically, far safer here. Embassy's riddled with bugs. However, I've booked the secure room there for you this afternoon. Now that your cover's complete, we move to Phase Two.'

Less bonhomie and more control evinced itself in Quinlevan's tone.

'You're now active. On return to Alexandria you're to make a test Morse transmission from the Consulate General at 11.00 local time Saturday. We'll be using the same type of one-time codebook that Scottie introduced you to. Here's your copy. I'd keep it in the consulate safe if I were you.'

'But what am I meant to do?'

'You're to work out a way to visit the port area regularly. Incognito in Egyptian dress. Aim is to report on naval shipping movements …'

'How?'

'How you find out the information is up to you. How you report to us depends. If you can, make sketches from memory and send them out via the consulate bag. I also have a piece of kit for you, which may come in handy if you get the opportunity. For ship types and numbers use Morse. After the initial contact we'll use this schedule to listen out for you so that your transmissions don't fall into a pattern. Memorise it now and return it to me.'

The major handed Nick a small card, which he twisted between sweaty fingers.

'Why? Why ships?'

'For years after the war we sold the Egyptians decommissioned Royal Navy vessels. Submarines too, for that matter. Did exactly the same for the Israelis. Balance, you see. But nowadays Nasser is getting his warships from the Soviet bloc. So we need to know what comes in and when.'

No messing about now. For real.

'You once said something about hiding in the open. Won't the Egyptians be on to me as soon as I transmit in Morse?'

'No one is going to expect it. A few bursts of high-speed transmission occasionally should go unnoticed. We'll reply only to your first message. You'll get your orders thereafter via the bag and the consulate. Anything really urgent, we'll send a Diplomatic Wireless Service message to Cairo.'

'I can sketch ships but won't have the faintest idea which ones you're interested in.'

'You will after this afternoon. No point in inducting you before – new types being introduced all the time. So when we're finished up here, you've got some homework to do in the embassy.'

'But what's happening in Egypt? People keep on saying something's going on.'

Quinlevan laid a firm hand on his arm.

'The balloon may go up or not. That's nothing for you to concern yourself with, my young man. Just get us the information we ask for and we'll handle it from there.'

'What about Bishop? Why did he leave so suddenly?'

'You've already asked me that. None of your business.'

'But surely others must know.'

Quinlevan sighed.

'Shall we just say he was caught with two sailors in a compromising position. Luckily, we were able to extract him before things got out of hand.'

A distance in the officer's tone forbade further probing.

On entry to the embassy basement secure room, Quinlevan passed him a small package with an encouraging wink.

'Leica. DDR makes the best lenses.'

He handed Nick over to the waiting technician.

'Don't bother with each other's names – just get on with it. Probably won't see me again until all this blows over. So chin up and best of luck, dear boy.'

Nick spent two hours in the darkened secure room, studying repeated monochrome projections of Soviet-bloc ships, tanks and missiles.

Tested, he did well, receiving a nod of approval from the technician.

Exhausted, waiting outside the embassy for a taxi to Ramses Station, he panicked. Couldn't do this. Madness. Would go back in and tell Quinlevan.

But he didn't.

CHAPTER 4

'Nick, my dear. You know I'll do anything you ask.'
'Well, actually, there is something, and I'm not at all sure how to put it.'

'Anything for you.'

Post-rehearsal in the soft warm air of the garden, Samy drank a glass of tea while Nick nursed a duty-free Scotch, courtesy of Col. He cleared his throat.

'Samy, I'm afraid it really won't work with you staying the night again.'

'But I don't understand – they all knew about Bishop and me.'

Nick paused, following the oily swirls of the malt in his glass. Richard had made him all too aware of the dangers of the course he was pursuing a little earlier that evening. 'There's the possibility of an extra performance in Cairo. But just wanted to share something with you first – hope you won't take it in the wrong way. We're all open-minded here, and with Bishop we most certainly had to be. But you should know that Samy is far from the most discreet of people. So your relationship is common knowledge in the department. Samy works in the Faculty Administration as well as being Professor Naguib's nephew. Basically, none of us want a repetition of the Bishop incident.'

'Which was?'

'Sudden and unpleasant.'

'Thank you – your advice and concern are much appreciated. And Cairo, why not? Bring it on.'

End of conversation.

In truth, he didn't really give a toss about the fate of the play, however much he enjoyed being with the cast. But suddenly, brilliantly, he could see a solution to the problem Quinlevan had set staring him in the face.

'Look, Samy, I don't actually care what they knew about you and Bishop. Frankly, that's history. But we cannot continue to meet here. Can't you see we need to find somewhere else to go – somewhere more discreet?'

Samy's face lightened as he brushed a lock of hair out of his eyes.

'Oh, a secret place?'

'Yes, that's right. Somewhere known only to the two of us – say a room down by Ras-El-Tin, for example.'

Samy rocked his head back to give him a shocked theatrical stare.

'That's quite a tough, I mean a very rough area.'

'I know, but no one will recognise us there.'

'It's not the kind of place that someone like me, let alone you, would go normally.'

'That's exactly why it's so perfect for us, my Samy. We can spend time together with no one knowing, or caring.'

'You just don't understand how difficult it could be.'

'It may be our only chance. Let's do it, my dear friend.'

'I can try, of course, but why not somewhere easier, more central?'

'Trust me, this is what I want for us. I'll pay for the room, of course, but you must first help find it. This idea means such a lot to me – and will to both of us, I hope.'

Samy remained mute for a painfully long moment, but finally grinned, delighted at being needed.

'Yes, of course, dear Nick.'

***

THE NEXT MORNING, THE 36 tram took them to Ras-El-Tin and they dived into the crowded streets near the docks. Friday prayers at the Abou-El-Abbas Mosque had just concluded. Children raced and screamed in the bright sunlight, bunches of men smoked and gossiped, and women chatted with half an eye on their offspring. Nick was acutely aware of being the only foreigner, and kept his gaze down so as not to meet curious stares.

'If you're with me, my dear, the price will be at least two or three times.'

They were in a teashop, discussing what to do, while three urchins in stained T-shirts stood just inside the doorway, staring in a friendly, curious, but persistent way. Under their scrutiny, Nick felt sweat trailing down his spine but resisted the futile desire to shoo them out. The only way forward was for Samy to scout the back streets alone.

'See you at the Elite at five.'

Nick passed through dark, narrow alleys, glanced up at sheets flapping from wooden balconies, and took in the scent of herbs and charcoal-grilled fish overlaying deeper odours.

However ethnically multi-layered Alexandria had once been, this area was now Arab through and through, with few traces of previous European influence.

***

'It's super. On a side street. Very discreet. Not too small, with a bed, table and chairs. For three months. Also four other rooms are rented there, so we may not be noticed.'

'The landlord?'

'Hassan understands that a friend and I need somewhere to stay from time to time.'

'What can I say, Samy? You've really come up trumps – thank you so much. And the galabeyas?'

'I found rough, second-hand ones, as you asked. They're already in the room, my dear.'

They decided to meet there at eight the following evening.

'Better first time in the dark, don't you think?'

***

The next morning, Nick went by arrangement to the Consulate General. On his return from Cairo he'd opened Quinlevan's package, which contained a small Leica SLR camera, eight rolls of black-and-white 35 mm film and a note.

> *Use whole roll each time. Do not develop. Take to CG for bag to London. Now burn this.*

He'd lit a match over the kitchen sink and done as instructed. Then he'd washed away the ashes. The camera and film had gone innocently into his top desk drawer. Hiding in the open.

Now, Col cupped his right hand around his ear.

'This building leaks. Get it, sunshine?'

The vice-consul had been waiting at the colonnaded entrance to the Consulate General and had taken him into his airy high-ceilinged office.

Behind it was a small windowless room, more a stationery cupboard really, with a ceiling-level ventilation grille through which a grey aerial wire disappeared. On a folding table in front of a lockable metal cupboard sat a Morse transmitter–receiver into which the aerial was plugged. A note was scrawled in pencil on the top sheet of a lined pad beside it:

> *Pre-set wavelengths for high-speed transmission after keying message. Aerial well concealed outside beneath plastic guttering – should reach Cyprus easily. Give me confidential items to take to Cairo for the bag. BOAC flight comes in just before midnight Wednesday, leaves early morning Thursday. I go down by train with our bag stuff in the evening, stay overnight, bring back what's come in. Need anything you have for London by 18.00 on Wednesdays.*

After Nick had read the message, Col tore it off the pad along with the blank sheet underneath in case of print-through, reached into the cupboard for a hand-cranked shredder, and fed both through it.

'Leave you to it. In my office.'

Having quickly encoded and keyed a test message, at 11.00 Nick pressed the transmit button, producing a high-pitched stream of almost indistinguishable dots and dashes. With headphones on, he hung in limbo until the set woke up again, producing a one-letter message, sent at normal speed, in clear.

. — .

dit-dah-dit
R
Received

His first transmission as a spy.

He restored the transmitter–receiver to the cupboard, retained the one-time pad, and fended off Col's well-meant invitation to drinks with a visiting War Graves delegation that evening.

On his return home, he half-skipped down the hill, whistling with relief before he was brought up short by the curious eyes of a pavement newspaper vendor.

***

'There, my dear, my *habibi*. What do you think?'

Samy pushed hard on the heavy door that had stuck, half-open, to reveal a bare single bed, a metal table with two sturdy upright chairs, a wardrobe with a cracked full-length door mirror, and a shuttered window overlooking a narrow side street. The door lacked a lock, and the room a carpet, curtains and linen. A bare bulb was the only illumination. While the floorboards were well swept, the furniture and walls betrayed a long-accumulated grime. However, the location close to the docks trumped everything. And he'd not the slightest intention of spending much time in the room itself.

Samy was elated, flinging open the wardrobe to reveal two rough, slightly used, dark-grey galabeyas, two pairs of flipflops – *shibshibs* – and two clean but discoloured headcloths.

'But what will Hassan think when he sees us dressed like this?'

'Nothing. He understands.'

Samy demonstrated how to wind the headcloth. Then, in the soft evening air, they wandered along narrow streets past brightly lit stalls. In a darker section, Samy took his hand briefly.

'That's normal here, *habibi*.'

Nick slowly relaxed, pleased to have apparently achieved invisibility; people accorded him no more than a passing glance.

After an hour's promenade they returned to the room. A moment's awkwardness hung in the air as they changed, but they left together in apparent harmony.

'That was wonderful, Samy. Can't thank you enough. See you at the rehearsal.'

'Not before?'

'No, I'm afraid not. Things to do.'

***

ON SUNDAY EVENING, HE returned to Ras-El-Tin. He slipped his key into the outside door and strode confidently upstairs to the room. Hassan called up after him from the hall and they exchanged greetings over the banisters.

Little point in keeping up the pretence of not understanding Arabic now.

He unwrapped the bundle he'd brought. After tossing sheets and towels on to the bed, he concealed his sketchpad and pencils under a pile of old newspapers at the bottom of the wardrobe.

He checked himself in the mirror, having carefully wound on the headcloth, before setting out into the dark streets.

Still getting his bearings in the maze of alleyways, but growing in confidence, he sought possible viewpoints for the docks.

Later, seated outdoors at a rickety café table, his hand shook as he sipped the glass of hot sweet tea. But no one showed any interest.

He'd come back earlier the next day while it was still light.

***

THE FOLLOWING MONDAY, NICK and Leila sat in the deserted staffroom during the mid-morning break. Leila ran through the procedure for the final-year examinations. Nick paid meticulous attention to her earnest explanations, struck by the graceful way she paused for comments.

Rachida, inevitably, held the key. She would type the questions on to stencils that Thursday and would then accompany them both to the Reproduction Room.

He kept a straight face and avoided eye contact with Leila. But when they shook hands at the end of the meeting, he might have held on for a little too long, judging by the flash in her eyes.

He hastened to the Faculty Administration for his official enrolment as an examiner and joined a short queue of academic staff. A low wooden railed bar divided the waiting area from the sea of clerks and their file-strewn desks.

At the head of the queue, a smiling Samy was handing Hans a university document in Arabic, topped with an embossed crest and purple date stamp.

Business done, Hans headed towards the door, halting abruptly beside him.

'What an excellent surprise! I wanted to get in touch with you for so long. We have new exhibition at the Cultural Centre. *Vernissage* is tomorrow at seven thirty. Can you come, please?'

There was little point in pretending he had a full social diary.

'Sure – thank you very much. Who's the artist?'

'Willi Sitte, our leading socialist realism painter.'

Nick had vaguely heard of the artist, though would have been hard pushed to define socialist realism.

'Great, that is wonderful. See you there.'

In due course, he was attended to by a rather subdued Samy.

'See you at the rehearsal on Thursday.'

'*I* didn't get invited to the opening of the exhibition.'

That boy really did have incredibly sharp hearing.

***

IN THE AFTERNOON, AT Ras-El-Tin Nick mingled at the entrance to the commercial port. Dockworkers flooded in and out whenever the barrier was raised for a truck.

With eyes lowered, he joined the next wave until they began to disperse. He walking alone and with purpose, only raising his head from time to time to glance at the naval docks now in plain view.

He had no need of a camera, instead snapping mental images of the craft lined up across the water. He didn't want to push his luck and soon joined a group of dockers heading towards the exit.

Outside the docks, he stopped twice to adjust his flipflops, as if to remove non-existent stones, and cast glances over his shoulder. Both times he glimpsed a figure stepping into the shadows. To be on the safe side, he doubled back on himself, eventually returning to the room a quarter of an hour later.

He fumbled with the headcloth. Little doubt about what would happen to him if caught – a beating the likely gentlest penalty. He pulled out his sketchpad, only for it to slip from his fingers to the floor. At that moment he understood it was not fear that was making him quiver, but excitement of the highest order.

He sat down at the table and composed himself, waiting for the tremors to pass, then took his sketchpad and drew outlines of the naval vessels he'd seen. He'd recognised some but not all. Now was not the time for identification, which he'd do at home; this was all about recall. He worked method-ically and left with two folded sheets of paper burning in his jacket pocket, a chill replacing his initial elation.

At home, he listed the types of vessel and converted the information into code: one T43-class Polish minesweeper, two Czech P-6 motor torpedo boats, two old Russian Sko-ry-class destroyers, three Russian W-class submarines and an unidentified frigate.

He burned the uncoded list in the kitchen sink, and put the sketches, coded list and one-time codebook into an envelope. He'd give the sketches to Col on Wednesday for the diplomatic bag.

Next, he pulled the large red *Dictionary of National Biography* from the bottom shelf of his bookcase and slid the envelope into a deep cavity he'd previously cut into the pages. Undoubtedly a risk, but he'd forbidden Hamid to interfere with his books.

***

ON TUESDAY AT 7.30 p.m. prompt, Nick presented himself at the DDR Cultural Centre, just off Saad Zaghloul. A black glass lift took him to the rooftop gallery where he joined the reception line. Hans greeted him warmly.

'Please to meet my wife. Frau Dr Dr Fussmann.'

Nick inclined his head and took the hand of a woman with steel-framed glasses, a pencil-thin mouth and the grip of a champion weightlifter.

He circulated; although he recognised a few faces from the university, he appeared to be the only member of the English Department. Two gin and tonics later, his personal reappraisal of socialist realism was interrupted by the clinking of spoon against glass. In English, Hans introduced the East German ambassador, who'd come down from Cairo to open the exhibition. Then he repeated the preamble in German and execrable Arabic.

'Well, hello there.'

His scrutiny of a Stakhovanite portrayal of glorious workers was interrupted by Grace and Col, both equipped with glasses of wine. Grace, in social mode, appeared to have had several.

'What do you make of this?' Before he could reply, Grace handed her husband an empty glass. 'Get me a refill, sweetie.'

She paused until Col had obediently moved off.

'Now, have to be quick. Got rid of Hans. Wanted to show me sexy etchings while wifey was at a party. Then rumpy-pumpy at his colleague's place.'

'Tomorrow night?'

'Eight.'

She let out a squeal of laughter as Col reappeared.

'Was just telling Nick about Hans. Claims he's got a box full of dirty drawings by Sitte, but the Egyptians won't let him display them! Thought they were the ones who invented *feelthy* pictures in the first place.'

'My love, people are looking at us.'

Col took her firmly by the forearm and the couple moved over to a less crowded corner of the room.

'Ah, Dr Hellyer, please to introduce our ambassador.'

Five minutes of diplomatic pleasantries followed.

'Sitte deserted Wehrmacht in 1944 to fight with Italian partisans.'

Eventually Hans put him out of his misery.

'Now I must introduce the ambassador to others, but take dinner with us after the reception, please. At the Union – I expect you heard of this restaurant.'

***

NICK ENTERED THE UNION through a discreet door off Old Bourse Street. He peered into a green leather-faced bar on the left, then headed for a high-ceilinged dining room to the right, dominated by a long, white linen-dressed table. Egyptian and DDR flags poked out from fresh floral decorations.

He consulted the table plan and he made his way to his seat between Frau Dr Dr Fussmann and a taciturn man from the city Highways Department.

Conversation was thus confined to discussion in French of traffic management enlivened by Frau Dr Dr's alarming practice of making random statements in English, before lapsing into silence.

'They say there will be desert storms soon.'

He'd accepted the invitation out of curiosity, but rapidly realised the food more than made up for the conversation. Saffron-flavoured bisque de crevettes preceded lobster, each mounted coachlike on a silver-plated tray seemingly drawn by langoustines attached by golden threads. Chateaubriand, with a deep Bordelaise sauce and Parmentier potatoes, was followed by harlequin soufflé.

The meal done, Nick excused himself from the table and headed for the kitchen. Photis, the Greek headwaiter, smiled as he opened the service door to reveal blackened cast-iron stoves, shining copper utensils, steam and flames. Three heavily built, white-clad and white-haired Nubian chefs ignored the intrusion.

'Trained in Switzerland in the 1920s.'

As the party broke up, he felt a steely grip on his upper arm. Frau Dr Dr.

'My husband tells me you are to return with us.'

He was marched off at speed to the DDR Cultural Centre, and out of breath when Hans caught up at the lift.

'Come in, so good of you. I wanted to offer you a drink. Do take a seat.'

Nick was led into a modest but tastefully furnished sitting room with an oddly out-of-place wooden crate in one corner.

'Excuse, please – have headache, so go to bed.'

As Frau Dr Dr disappeared, Hans waved two large cognac glasses and a bottle in the air.

'Good, easier for us men to talk.'

As the night wore on and the level in the bottle sank, Hans became ever more companionable and indiscreet.

'See that box over there? Go have a look. By Sitte. But you don't recognise them, no? Of course, the Egyptians don't let me display them here.'

Nick carefully flicked through the pictures – striking erotic drawings and paintings, clearly by the same artist and executed with great sensitivity.

'Shame not to show them – but surely the Egyptians must decide in their own country.'

'But whose land is it really? That's the question. Used to be yours, no? Perhaps you Britishers want Egypt back. After all, Nasser took your Suez Canal. Who knows what you want? If there wouldn't so many secrets, the world would be a much safer place, don't you think?'

Hans sloshed cognac into their glasses.

'Thank you very much. Well, I'm solidly against the atomic bomb. And I'm completely anti-war, you know. Against secrets, too.'

'Stands to reason. If there wouldn't be any secrets, there wouldn't be any wars. You can see from that box of pictures, people are same anywhere. You know from the dinner tonight that we, the people of the DDR, also appreciate the finer things in life.'

Hans leaned forward and waved his glass.

'But do the British appreciate you? How much do they pay you as a lecturer? Not much I guess – that's typical. Have you ever thought of supplementing it? Of making another little income?'

'Well, no, not really. I suppose I wouldn't know how to. You mean giving private lessons, that kind of thing?'

'Not exactly so. But perhaps you might like to co-operate with us in a friendly way. So, for example, we could compensate you for passing on small informations. I happen to know you are sometimes in the consulate and the embassy. You could inform us of any gossips you hear. That kind of thing – who's visiting, who they're seeing – all in the name of peace, of course.'

'I suppose there'd be nothing wrong with that, as you say. Just a bit of gossip, tittle-tattle. So why not?'

'Excellent! We will pay you in US dollars. Shall we arrange to meet once a week? Absolutely no reason for you not to visit here. After all, it is a free country. No?'

Hans enjoyed his little joke so much that he almost choked on the spirit.

When they'd drained the bottle, Nick took a taxi home and collapsed into bed fully dressed. He lay with unseeing, wide-open eyes. Surely, come the morning, the German would dismiss their discussion as flippant. But if not, what had Nick done by agreeing to co-operate?

***

NICK AWOKE WITH A parched mouth, blinding headache and no appetite. What he'd done was all too alarming.

Later, on returning from the university, he retrieved his codebook from the DNB and wrote an account for Quinlevan, which he transmitted on schedule along with his report on shipping.

'Many thanks, Col. Here's my envelope for London. Have a good trip.'

'What are you doing tonight, sunshine? Grace'll be all on her own, you know, so why not pop in? Be good if she wasn't on her tod all evening.'

'Yes, of course – delighted.'

***

AT EIGHT, GRACE FLUNG open the door of the flat in the Dafrawi Building before he could knock.

'Heard the lift. Now, what drink is my man going to tempt me with?'

A sweep of her arm indicated a comprehensive range of duty-free spirits on the sideboard.

Knowledge acquired on the *Esperia* came in handy, and he constructed two Negronis from equal parts of gin, sweet red vermouth and Campari.

Graced tasted hers, then kicked off her shoes before sweeping the rest down.

'Wow! That hits the spot. Another one, please. And how was the dinner last night, by the way? Did you go on anywhere afterwards?'

He sketched in the evening, omitting Hans's final proposition. She tittered at first and then laughed out loud.

Nick stroked her forearm.

'Like classical music? Hope so because you're going to hear some now.'

She lowered the stylus on to an LP already sitting on a portable Dansette record player. Handel's *Messiah* blared out as she lay down with her head in his lap, cupping her right ear just as Col had done.

'Now we can say and do whatever we want.'

She pulled at his beard, then ran her fingers over his face.

'Lie there and I'll replay for you everything we did together last time,' he whispered.

She chuckled and closed her eyes, her right hand pulling up her dress and her forefinger sliding in between her legs. He carefully revisited their lovemaking as she rubbed her head against him.

End of the first side of the LP.

Finger to her lips, she stood and yanked her panties three quarters of the way up. Then she unplugged the Dansette, picked it up and lurched off.

He followed her crab-like progress down a long corridor to a plush bedroom. Efficiently, she lowered the blinds, put the music back on, stripped off and lay on the silk sheets.

'I'm yours, darling. Take me.'

He did. A lustful equality he'd never experienced before.

'Well, you do give a girl a good time.'

She gave a throaty laugh and slapped him on the buttocks playfully but hard enough to sting.

'Come on – that always makes me hungry. Bring the music.'

They trotted back to the lounge with the record player and perched naked on the sofa, eating French bread and strong garlicky cheese with glasses of white Burgundy.

'You know, this diplomatic life isn't too bad on occasion. But can you imagine the parade of my days? Dinners like the one you had last night. Treated like an appendage. Followed.'

'I'd follow you.'

'Bugged. Can't have my children with me. Can't even pick

my own lovers. Col's a good guy and I won't hear anything against him. But, let's put it this way, he ain't too imaginative in the sack. Hans was a brief distraction. But I had the feeling that he was fucking me to get at Col, if you know what I mean.'

What had she meant – not choosing her lovers? As for Hans, possibly the other way round. And what about himself?

The phone in the entrance lobby rang.

'Col – couldn't say much, of course. Bag came in very early so already on his way back. By car, not train. Stopped part way to ring. Seems there's a bit of a flap. Best you go.'

***

HE WALKED SLOWLY DOWN Kafr Abdou. As he brushed a mosquito away from his face he caught her intimate scent.

He crossed the avenue at the bottom of the hill and stepped out in front of a puttering unlit motorcycle. The rider swerved, wobbled and contrived to avoid him, his pillion passenger leaving behind a trail of curses.

CHAPTER 5

ALERTED BY THE BLAST of the Land Rover's horn, Nick came flying out of the house into the crowd of giggling, white-bloused, dark-skirted girls who'd quickly surrounded the vehicle. It was 7.30 a.m.

'Good morning, Said.'

'Morning, sir. Lovely morning. Vice-consul want to see you now, sir. Urgent.'

He returned to the house, downed his coffee, retrieved his codebook, and dived into the front seat in under a minute. Said got under way, carefully navigating the parting sea of schoolgirls.

Col must have twigged about him and Grace. He was clearly heading for the outraged-deceived-husband-and-pistols-at-dawn scene.

'Got mail for you. But, first, come for a walk.'

As usual in crisp shirt and brown brogues, but uncharacteristically business-like, Col offered no chitchat or bad puns.

With trepidation, Nick followed the vice-consul out of the back door of the Consulate General and into the garden of the adjoining Residence. The gravel paths and fine display of roses had been tended by Edith Winks with a passion she did not accord to her husband.

'Something to tell you, Nick, and this is the place to do it.'

Col had never used his first name before. No longer 'sunshine', he feared the worst.

'Pretty sure the garden ain't bugged – old Prague story about the cunning Czechs taping little microphones to the roses along the path of the ambassador's regular afternoon walks. Sure Edith would've noticed if it'd been done here though.'

This was more like the Col he knew.

'Got two DWS communications for you marked *Top Urgent*. Security classification on one of them is way above my level, so had to return last night by embassy car.'

'Right, yes, I see.'

Although he didn't. While uneasy with Col's slight air of deference, he was secretly delighted that the topic was not the one he'd feared.

Col passed over two sealed envelopes.

'Leave you to it, then.'

The first, shorter, message was in reply to his Morse transmission.

> *Good start. Look out for R-class submarines. 3 being delivered this year. Also Komar-class guided-missile patrol boats. Send more drawings and if possible photos in next bag. Also look out for cargo vessels from Poland and DDR. Q*

Straightforward. He remembered the differences between the W-class and the later R-class submarines, and the Komar was pretty unmistakable.

The second message was heavier stuff altogether.

Useful potentially valuable approach. Could be significant but need to be sure not provocation. In future communications refer to contact as 'Treadmill'. Agree to your meeting him on Tuesday. Supply true information you know about consulate and embassy. He needs to trust you so all must be checkable. Refer to meeting of Middle East defence attachés on day you were in Cairo but make no reference to secure room. He may not know about the meeting but his superiors certainly will. Have to breed faith in you as a source. Be aware that whatever venue is chosen for the meeting it will certainly be bugged. Communicate as per schedule. Report embassy a week tomorrow for face-to-face briefing. Acknowledge receipt and destroy. Q

Quinlevan was taking Hans's drunken offer far too seriously for Nick's liking. How to handle an agent had most definitely not been on the menu at MECAS. Yes, he'd visit the DDR Cultural Centre on Tuesday afternoon, but very much doubted if Herr Director would have much recall of the evening.

Back in the consulate he shredded the messages, transmitted a brief coded acknowledgement of receipt and handed over his one-time pad, with a mime of opening and closing the office safe, having decided that keeping it at home now was too dangerous.

Col caught his glance at the pile of London newspapers on the desk.

'Consul General gets them first, does all the blasted cross-words, then passes them on to me. Tell you what though, we're going out to Agami on Sunday with George. The Winks boy, you know? Here over half-term. Why not come along and grab the papers then? And would you like Said to drop you off at your house in a minute?'

'Agami would be great. But I don't need a lift home, thank you. It *is* downhill, you know!'

**

LEILA WAS WAITING IN the corridor outside Rachida's office and flashed a quick, nervous smile before sharing her contribution to the examination paper.

'Great questions – right on the spot and will make them think before answering. And no need to worry about your English at all – certainly much more correct than mine.'

Rachida glanced at his offering, then rapped the sheets of paper hard on her desk to bring them into alignment.

'I am obliged to inform you, Dr Hellyer, that your handwriting is virtually illegible.'

She typed the examination paper on to stencils at a metronomic speed, pausing only once to rectify an error with bright-pink correcting fluid.

'And now to the Reproduction Room.'

Rachida slipped on a housecoat-like grey overall and led them to the end of a tiled corridor. She ceremoniously unlocked a cramped room containing a manual Gestetner machine, a table with a tray of large ink-spattered plastic bottles and a pile of boxes containing duplicating paper. An adjoining WC had been converted into an improvised incineration facility. Inside was a blackened dustbin with holes drilled into its sides and a small metal chimney in the middle of its lid. It balanced precariously on the edges of the toilet bowl.

'Right! Twenty-five copies of each page, all to be numbered by hand after printing. You keep one copy and I hold the other twenty-four until examination day. Any badly printed copies and the stencils themselves to be burnt. Okay?'

She fitted the first stencil into the machine, squirted in ink from one of the plastic bottles, inserted a pile of paper and turned the handle. The first half-dozen came out barely legible or too smudgy, but with steady turning, clean copies began to emerge. Rachida seemed oblivious to the stench of the ink, or to the squelch it made as it was forced through the stencil on to paper.

'There. Now remember – burn the spoiled ones and stencils when you've finished. I'm afraid I can't hang around – too much to do.' She touched Leila on the arm and gave a slight smile. 'I'm pretty sure you'll be safe with him.'

Rachida left the Reproduction Room, closing the door firmly behind her and locking it. Nick raised an eyebrow and grinned at Leila.

'Let's get on with it, then. I'll turn the handle if you like.'

In such a confined space it was inevitable they'd brush against each other, that their hands would touch. The first few times one or the other apologised, but then it became a natural rhythm.

'There.'

She removed the final stencil from the Gestetner, dripping all over the floor.

'Oh, no!'

He looked down at her stained gold slippers; there was little to be done. He was already regretting wearing a decent short-sleeved white shirt, which was now spotted with presumably indelible duplicator ink.

Nick screwed up the spoiled papers into balls in the WC, while Leila numbered the finished ones in the duplicator room. With the dustbin almost full of paper, he piled the stencils on top and tried to ignite the incinerator from a hole near the bottom using a couple of matches. Nothing happened. So he reformed one of the paper balls into a long spill. When it was well lit, he took off the lid and tossed it in.

A sudden *oomph* half-deafened him and a searing flash burnt off most of the hairs on his right forearm. In panic, he forced the lid back on. A steadily thickening stream of malodorous black smoke billowed from the chimney, swiftly spreading to the duplicator room and bringing Leila hurtling in.

'Quick, the window! Before we choke.'

The gap between the increasingly hot metal bin and the wall was narrow, but Leila was decisive.

'Lift me up. I can open it.'

Clouds of stinking fumes now filled the air as Leila launched herself from his arms. With one hand she grasped the cords dangling from the high window, then fell back, dragging it down and open. Nick grabbed hold of her just before she hit the incinerator and pulled her away.

Coughing and spluttering in the suffocating heat, he held her tight to his chest, stroking her hair soothingly. Slowly her head tilted back and he gently kissed her forehead. She gave a deep sigh then reached up and pulled him down to her lips.

Oblivious, they were interrupted by a cry from the direction of the Gestetner. Rachida was among them again.

Nick rushed back first, his right arm stretched out to guide him through the pitch-black, but when his hand encountered an ample bosom, inducing a squawk, he hastily pushed Leila ahead.

'Oh, how terrible. Are you both okay? I knew I should have stayed here. It's all my fault. I completely forgot to tell you about the ventilation window.'

After Rachida had carried off her twenty-four copies, they cleaned themselves off as best they could.

'About a little while ago—'

She shook her head. 'Don't. Words aren't useful. What happened, happened. That's a fact and I don't regret it. Do you? We have to work out what to do about that moment, that's all.'

He recalled her earlier decisiveness.

'I hardly know you, although I'm aware of the rumours and may or may not believe them. Best to leave things as they are for now.'

'Right, then. So until the rehearsal tonight?'

'Yes, naturally.'

He caught her shining eyes as she walked briskly out of the staffroom. He moved to the window and waited until she appeared again, heading past the palm trees towards the sea.

Back home, he put his reeking clothes out for Hamid to launder, though with little hope for the white shirt. Soot swirled in his bathwater and disappeared down the plughole.

He'd hoped to keep in touch with the news on his new

portable radio but had been disappointed. Constant short-wave retuning had only twice yielded the notes of 'Lilliburlero', followed by 'This is London calling.' Instead, he'd come to rely on the *Egyptian Gazette*, published daily in Cairo with agency world-news stories, reports of Egyptian events, including cultural ones, and notices of shipping movements. Seeing the London newspapers again on Sunday would be a bit of a culture shock.

***

'And you should have seen Rachida's face!'

At the rehearsal, Leila treated everyone to a dramatic account of the inferno in the Reproduction Room, getting her story out ahead of the inevitable gossip.

The cast turned to the scene in hand and, with prompts from Mamdouh, Richard led them through it. Not exactly method acting, as every movement and reaction was scripted in lengthy stage directions.

During the tea-cum-cigarette break, Samy, Sohail and Samira, eager for more details, surrounded Leila. Nick meanwhile sat on the front terrace overlooking the street with Lucky, who'd lit a Cleopatra.

'Join me?'

Nick shook his head.

'You're very different from Bishop, you know.'

Lucky blew smoke rings, looked around and leaned forward.

'Couldn't keep his eyes or his hands off me. After rehearsals I'd have him on his knees, begging.'

'Why are you telling me this?'

Lucky looked across at him from the deep-cushioned bamboo chair in which he was half-lying.

'Because I've been watching you with Leila, and seen the same look in your eyes. You should know that she has a long-term boyfriend – Abdul El Salem, ten years older, an army officer with very high-up connections.'

'What are you trying to tell me?'

'If you and Leila get together and Abdul finds out, I wouldn't want to be either of you. Particularly not you. Anyway, what's wrong with Samira?'

At the end of rehearsal, Nick and Richard lounged over a drink on the garden swing. Nick came inside to replenish the whisky supplies and surprised Samy at the bookshelves with the *Dictionary of National Biography* in his hands.

'Look – someone's vandalised your book! Who would do such a thing?'

'Don't know. Had it for years and never looked at it. Best to chuck it out then. Now, would you like to join us?'

'No, my dear. You know I don't drink.'

'Sorry, course not.'

He took the bottle of Scotch into the garden where Richard was sitting straight-backed with the air of someone about to make an important announcement.

'Looks as if Cairo may be on but we need to firm things up with the American University – their campus theatre is quite central. Mamdouh and I could go up next Thursday afternoon and come back on Friday.'

'Ooh, can I come Richard?'

Little escaped Samy, who'd come out on to the terrace.

'Sure. Only two spare beds in my friend's flat though, so

it would mean sleeping on the floor.'

'Oh, perhaps not, then. See you tomorrow, Nick?'

'Yes, of course. Looking forward to it. Midday.'

Nick saw his two guests out and sank back on the sofa, the shock of the morning's event still coursing through his body.

***

THE NEXT DAY, HE and Samy mingled with the crowds, eating slow-cooked beans and lightly spiced falafel. As they strolled, Samy seemed at ease and chatted happily. Nick smiled and responded, but kept his thoughts to himself.

He had to do something to bring Samy closer to him, because without the room here he'd be lost. A big gesture, perhaps; a shared secret.

On their return, as they ate sweetmeats bought from an ancient white-painted barrow, Nick cracked it.

'Let me sketch you.'

Samy was predictably delighted.

'Naked.'

Samy responded with alacrity, lying on the bed, his legs drifting apart.

'No, not like that.'

Nick proceeded to guide Samy: seated with his back to him, head turned slightly over his right shoulder and bowed, hands on thighs. The directions were precise, and in Arabic.

Samy began to do as he was instructed, then stopped and swung around, open-mouthed.

'Arabic?'

'You heard me – now take up the pose.'

He sketched carefully for half an hour, concentrating on the nape of the neck and the curves of the upper body. He was pleased with the completed drawing, as was the subject, who asked if he could keep it.

'Of course, my friend. But the language – that's something that stays between us. No one else knows.'

'But how did you—?'

'Of course, one day I'll share that secret with you. But from now on when we're alone, let's use Arabic together. And you can teach me to speak better – I'm really only a beginner.'

Samy beamed and asked Nick to sign the sketch with love. Which he did – before explaining that he wasn't sure when they could be together again.

Samy sulked a little but, seemingly buoyed up with the new intimacy, agreed that 'soon' was the best they could hope for.

***

THE NEXT DAY AT noon, Nick was back at the docks, having learned from the *Egyptian Gazette* that the *Esperia* was due. This time he was in European clothes on a terrace near the top of the maritime station packed with waving friends and relatives; it afforded him a much clearer view into the naval part of the harbour.

***

ON SUNDAY AT TEN, he climbed into the back seat of Grace's car and sat next to the consul general's seventeen-year-old son, George. The podgy youth, who combined a mop of ginger hair with a rather sullen expression, ignored him completely, only perking up when Grace glanced back to make some observation about a passing feature.

On arrival at Agami, Col took him aside.

'About your trip to Cairo this week. Been asked to provide transport – don't ask me why. Train's always been good enough for my humble self. So Said will take you up on Thursday afternoon, back on Friday.'

'That's really kind. Thank you very much.'

Over a leaden al-fresco lunch, Nick tried to liven things up by recounting amusing things from the rehearsals.

'Went to one of their productions last year, didn't we, Col? Tennessee Williams, wasn't it? *Cat on a Hot Tin Roof.*'

'Well, this year we're doing a black comedy by a young Egyptian playwright.'

'Why not perform it in Arabic, then? Why translate, I mean?'

Nick glanced at the teenager.

'Good question, George. Dunno. Whatever – we're putting the play on here, and then probably in Cairo.'

Grace passed him the salad bowl.

'You're going up to Cairo at the end of the week, aren't you, Nick?'

'Actually, just occurred to me. Don't suppose it's at all possible, Col, but I wondered about me giving the director and writer a lift. They need to suss out a venue there. Would quite understand if it isn't on, of course.'

'Sure. Something to think about. Who are they?'

'I'm sure you know Richard, the director. Mamdouh, the writer, is an ex-student – not sure what his subject was.'

'The Egyptian may not want to accept a lift, you know. Locals are discouraged from fraternising with us diplomatic lot. Nothing at all against the idea of you giving him a ride but you may find he gets cold feet.'

After lunch, Col and George went out for a run. Nick and Grace exchanged glances.

'They'll be a little while. Think I don't know – all they do is jog up the beach a kilometre to a small bar. Honestly – boys! Come on!'

Afterwards, they lay quietly in each other's arms.

'Poor little Georgie Porgie's got a bit of a crush on me. Haven't given him any encouragement. Not much anyway. Seventeen-year-olds – on a hair-trigger, if you know what I mean.'

They were sitting companionably, leafing through the English papers, when the 'boys' returned. George, eager to have Grace's attention, was delighted to share the back seat with her on their return in the gathering darkness.

***

On Tuesday, Nick presented himself at the DDR Cultural Centre and it became immediately and chillingly obvious that Hans had total recall of their previous conversation.

'So good to see you. So very glad you decided we could do business together.'

Rising from his desk, the German suggested they take tea in the roof garden, as it would be easier to talk there. But Quinlevan's warning resonated.

Hans led the way upstairs.

'Before, this building belonged to an English merchant and was sequestrated after Suez. The hall where you visited the Sitte exhibition last week used to be a dancing floor, a sprung ballroom. This garden itself was made by the merchant with plants from his own country. So you can see that in today's Egypt, we Chermans are becoming the new English.'

Nick smiled politely, drank his Earl Grey tea from a Wedgwood porcelain cup while eating Marie biscuits, and prepared to betray his country.

As instructed, he related what he knew about the embassy and Consulate General staff and premises, omitting all reference to the secure room. Hans questioned him closely about the meeting of defence attachés. When Nick added that a UN observer had been there, Hans wanted to know whom. Nick told him. Then the questions turned to the state of Col and Grace's marriage, and the answer was that as far as Nick knew it was rock solid.

'I have ways of checking these things. Thank you. Is there any more? No? Let us say the same time next week, then?'

Five minutes later and a hundred dollars richer, Nick left the DDR Cultural Centre.

So this was what real spying was about. Being paid twice to tell lies.

***

ON WEDNESDAY, HE MADE another clandestine visit to the docks, as Grace was entertaining George at a card evening.

He scored an R-class submarine and two Czech P6 motor torpedo boats. No need to entrust the sketches to Col as he was going to Cairo himself.

He returned to the room by a circuitous route, fairly sure he hadn't been tailed. The possibility only heightened the buzz.

CHAPTER 6

As predicted, Mamdouh had turned down the lift to Cairo so Richard had offered it to Samy, who'd agreed with delight.

'What fun! I've never been in a diplomatic car.'

Early on Thursday morning, beyond Lake Mariout a narrow ribbon of tarmac stretched out in front of them. As the kilometres passed, the landscape changed from shale-like rock outcrops to barren stony ground. Soon Said picked up speed on the empty road and all Nick could see were dunes from which sand drifted like thin clouds of smoke. He turned to the driver.

'No sign of anyone out here.'

'Sometimes Bedouin with camels, sir. But no see.'

Just then, atop a dune, they found themselves heading straight towards a camel in the middle of the road, its long neck bowed down towards them.

The massive head smashed straight through the windscreen.

Struggling for air, Nick eyeballed an astonished dromedary whose rotting deep yellow teeth were ringed by curled, bleeding lips. Nick was horrified; the animal was still very much alive. Its head twisted and jerked violently from side to side as the jagged windscreen edges ripped its neck open. A fierce spray of rust-red blood drenched him and a terrible roaring bellow filled his ears.

The dying beast's yellow-flecked eyes rolled. Halitosis filled Nick's consciousness until the thrashing and the cacophony abruptly ceased. Only then did he become aware of the steady drip-drip of blood from the dashboard and the rhythmic ticking of the cooling engine.

'All right, sir?'

'Yes. Not hurt. You?'

'Thanks be to God.'

The driver's voice had gone up a pitch, putting the lie to his assurance. Nick peered back over the leather bench seat to find Samy cowering in the footwell, and a white-faced Richard staring fixedly ahead. Both were lightly blood-splattered; neither uttered a word.

Said restarted the engine, jammed the steering column gearshift into reverse, revved the engine hard and let the clutch out abruptly. The car leapt backwards, dislodging the camel's head from the windscreen. Its neck slipped down the bonnet, momentarily catching on the stubby flagstaff before falling to the ground.

As the car jerked to a halt, the beast's head was replaced by the bearded faces of two men with pockmarked skin, wearing filthy beige headcloths. Smearing blood off the side window with his sleeve, Nick came face-to-face with two more Bedouin unsheathing long wooden-handled knives.

Said rocketed the car back again; the men on the bonnet scrabbled for grip before sliding off on to the road. He continued reversing until they were a good ten metres away, and climbed out. Head held high and shoulders pulled back, he took giant strides towards the four Bedouin.

The men roared at him, gesticulating at the camel and the car. Nick caught *miyya khamseen gnee*, a hundred and fifty pounds. Said stood rock still in his besmirched uniform, arms folded as the storm raged around him. The furious Bedouin continued to wave their knives as Said stared down at them in ominous silence. In the apparent absence of any response to their anger, all four moved to bypass the driver and headed towards the car.

At that moment, Said gave out a great cry, grabbing the nearest man by the neck of his long shirt with one hand and holding him up so they were eyeball to eyeball. Letting out a tirade of abuse, he shook the man, pointing to the camel, then the vehicle, with his free hand.

'He's demanding five hundred pounds for damage to the car.' Samy, enthralled, had crept up to peep over the back of the front bench seat.

Said was incandescent and the other men fell back a little, returning knives to sheaths and belts. Behind them in a dip in the dunes, Nick could see a line of laden camels tended by three veiled Bedouin women and their open-mouthed children.

Said thrust the man away from him. The Bedouin fell to the ground on his back beside the dying beast and stretched out his hand, demanding payment. Then he got to his feet, spat contemptuously and moved to join the others. The standoff continued, with Said adamant and the Bedouin threatening wildly.

An occasional overloaded car passed, crawling cautiously through the sand to avoid the crash scene. Faces glued to the windows stared out at them, rubber-necking but not wanting to get involved.

From over the next rise, a khaki police jeep with flapping side curtains and a flashing blue light appeared in a cloud of dust. The uniformed driver and an officer got out, the latter pulling on a peaked cap to show his authority. They were immediately surrounded by the Bedouin.

The officer listened carefully but didn't respond. He marched over to the car and enquired as to the passengers' identities. Said introduced Nick and Richard as important foreign university professors and emphasised the diplomatic status of the vehicle. A handful of notes passed between driver and policeman.

The officer marched briskly back to the Bedouin and announced his decision. *Ishreen gnee.* Twenty pounds.

After token resistance, the men accepted the money and signalled to the women, who came running up the dune with baskets and drawn knives. The policemen watched over the butchery of the dying animal and were rewarded with a large hunk of meat wrapped in a sack and deposited in the jeep.

Back at the car, Said wound a cloth around his right fist and smashed out the rest of the windscreen.

'We go now, sir, while policemen still here.'

As they drove off, Nick peered back through the rear window at the flashing blue light, so incongruous in that timeless desert scene of life and death.

'Grateful for what you did, Said. But don't quite under-stand what happened back there.'

'Simple, sir.'

The driver squinted against the blast of air.

'Officer, poor man. From fifty pounds I give him, Bedouin get twenty, he keep rest.'

The Zodiac limped the thirty kilometres back to Alexandria. Nick pulled his jacket up over his head, less to keep warm and more to shield himself from the dust and insects, as Said steered the silent stricken car home through increasingly heavy traffic.

***

NICK PUSHED STRAIGHT PAST a shocked Hamid and stripped off in the bathroom to rid himself of the stench of blood.

He lay back in his second colourful bath of the week, fending off recurrent images of the camel's head bursting through the windscreen. He could hear Hamid downstairs, cross-examining the other two as flecks of blood were sponged from their clothes.

Half an hour later, strengthened by stiff gin and tonics, Nick, Richard and Samy shared sandwiches in the sitting room.

Having hardly said a word since the accident, Richard blurted out, 'Close-run thing that – thought we were goners.'

The subsequent silence was shattered by repeated hooting. Nick dashed out to greet a mini-convoy led by Ibrahim and Col in the Land Rover, with Grace in her yellow Viva behind.

Col leapt down from the Land Rover, thumping him on the shoulders.

'Nick, you young devil. Really did for the consul general's car, didn't you?'

'Said was magnificent – saved us.'

'Good show. Told you he was a brick. Now, thing is, desert road's not too clever after dark. Need to get going now. Grace will drive, but you'd better leave at once.'

'Grace?'

'She offered. My masters in Cairo seem happy – better option for them than the train, apparently. So off you go and come back in one piece tomorrow.'

Nick called the others. Grace knew Richard but Samy required an introduction.

'Oh, you must come and sit with me – you can spill all the beans about the mysterious Dr Hellyer.'

Col waved them off, Samy bolt upright in the front seat.

Nick looked out for, but failed to recognise the site of the accident beneath the sheets of sand sweeping across the road. Camels and Bedouin had vanished into the vast expanse of the Western Desert.

The single-carriageway desert road wasn't busy; most traffic used the more direct Delta route. Grace drove the two hundred and twenty kilometres at an even speed, only easing up when they were overtaken by packed Peugeot 505 estates with heavily laden roof racks.

'Smugglers from Libya.'

Soon they were entering Giza and the outlines of the Great Pyramid and the Sphinx appeared in the fading late afternoon sunlight. A dispiriting ribbon of villas, low-rise apartments, shops and cafés led them into the centre of Cairo.

'Good late-night clubs out this way – been to a couple.'

She negotiated a gaggle of donkey carts before dropping Richard and Samy off near Tahrir Square. Then she parked the car in the embassy and vanished inside to make a call to Alexandria, while Nick checked into the Nile Hotel.

***

'SO WHO ARE WE meeting at this place in Zamalek?'

Shimmering lights from the island were reflected in the slow-flowing broad river.

'Mitri Amin from the Cairo Opera House. He's a friend of Richard's with good American University contacts.'

'With the greatest respect, darling, don't think your amateur dramatics are quite up to Opera House standard.'

She raised an eyebrow as she drained her glass and signalled for another.

'And don't turn your nose up at this stuff – the Egyptians were growing vines two thousand years before the French even thought of it.'

At the restaurant, they perched on stools under trees until the others turned up soon after eight. Mitri turned out to be a complete charmer, taking a flirtatious Grace under his wing and carrying the men along with him by sheer force of personality. His bald brown pate and hooded eyes shone as he entertained them with anecdotes, which may or may not have been true.

'Tomorrow we do business with the AUC and they will say yes. But tonight, after dinner, I'll give you a treat.'

The waves of barbecued meat that arrived at the table under the semi-darkness tasted delicious. However, Nick didn't recognise the cuts and irrationally hoped the meat wouldn't turn out to be camel.

'And these are?'

'All from sheep. Heart, lungs, liver, stomach. Here, try some more.'

Mitri took a fresh tray from a waiter's hands and served everyone. Nick chewed a couple of what appeared to be kidneys, but that had a distinctive light flavour and delicate texture.

Mitri smiled broadly. 'Good? Balls – sheep testicles.'

Grace pronged a forkful.

'Glad you like this place. It's really quite famous and people say our president is a great fan.'

Grace touched Mitri's arm. 'Is he really as popular as people say?'

'How can I answer that? You must understand that we Egyptians use jokes to cope with the absurdities of life. Recently Gamal Abdul ordered a crackdown and, after trawling the bazaars, the secret police pulled in a tall Nubian joke-smith and brought him to the president. "Are you the person who dares to make fun of me like this?" Nasser retold a joke. "Yes, that's one of mine." The Nubian proudly gave the same answer as our increasingly irritated president retold several more. "But don't you know that I was elected by ninety-nine per cent of the Egyptian people?" The Nubian doubled up with laughter. "That's hysterical. But it's not one of mine!"'

After dinner, Mitri took them on a surely illicit late-night tour of his beloved Opera House.

'Built to mark the opening of the Suez Canal. The premiere of Verdi's *Aida* took place here in 1871.'

Having arranged to pick up Richard and Samy for the drive back to Alexandria at two the following afternoon, they returned to the Nile Hotel.

Grace patted his arm.

'Well, my lover, I'm whacked. See you in the morning.'

***

NICK STOOD IN THE darkness on the balcony, naked and disappointed, until the attentions of persistent mosquitoes eventually forced his retreat.

A peremptory rap.

He grabbed a sheet from the bed in panic before opening the door to Grace, who was clutching a bottle of chilled sparkling wine.

'Think I'd pass up an opportunity like this?'

She kicked the door shut behind her, put down the tray and, reaching up under his sheet, gave him an affectionate squeeze.

***

AT FIVE O'CLOCK IN the morning, two thunderous booms followed by the crash of shattered windows jolted them awake. Disorientated, Nick lunged out of bed to open the balcony shutters, grateful that he'd failed to close their inner glass doors. Peering down, he could see confused, partly dressed hotel guests spilling out on to the glass-littered street.

None the wiser, he returned to the warm curve of Grace's back.

'Don't know what that was. Some kind of gas explosion, I suppose. No need for us to evacuate anyway.'

Soon, but not too soon, she returned to her room.

***

AT BREAKFAST, SHE EXPLAINED that she was going to spend the morning in the Khan El Khalili, the great souk.

'Don't pigeonhole me as a shopper. Just been to the Egyptian Museum too many times. See you back here for lunch.'

As it was a Friday the embassy gates were closed. After repeated rings, a uniformed guard finally opened up and, having checked Nick's identity, escorted him to the basement secure room where Quinlevan awaited.

'Didn't expect to see you so soon again, dear boy. Take a pew and tell me all about your new best friend, Hans.'

Nick related everything he could recall about the East German, from the chance meeting on the *Esperia* to Tuesday's rooftop conversation. Quinlevan nodded from time to time.

'So that was just fortune, then, bumping into him on the ship, I suppose.'

'What else could it be?'

'You see, your Hansie is known to us. Know why he is Dr Dr? Second degree an honorary one from a Pakistani university – very helpful to them he was with their research into all things atomic. Came to Egypt from Karachi, and before that worked in Rio de Janeiro. Same cover, university lecturer, cultural institute. Tries to recruit agents – indeed, as he's just recruited you.'

'I see.'

'Do you think he believed what you told him on Tuesday?'

'Well, I hope so because it was the truth.'

'Good. Had to be checkable, by him or his superiors. Truth's a bit of a theme with us, you see, young Nick. You came to us for a different role. Never intended you as a double agent. So you must believe me implicitly and do exactly what I say. How do you feel about that?'

An attempt at a confident smile.

'Now, the first thing you must do is always tell me the truth. That word again. And you haven't. You've lied twice already today – sins of omission perhaps, but still not giving me the whole picture. We cannot proceed if you hold things back.'

Quinlevan sank back in his chair with a weary, tolerant smile.

'You and I both know that's not what I'm asking about. Now is the moment for you to admit how things really are.'

He really couldn't tell Quinlevan about Grace. Yes, a free spirit and unlike anyone he'd ever known. And, yes, she could look after herself. And, yes, he was aware of an ambiguity in their relationship.

'Will make it easier for you. Someone with nothing to hide would have started our conversation today rather differently. An account of, not to mention a query about, the enormous booms you heard at five o'clock this morning. You didn't. Why not?'

Quinlevan knew.

'Because you were in bed with Mrs Dudley. True, or not?'

'Yes.'

'What woke you were two Israeli Mirage III jets sweeping over the desert before flying up the Nile. Came through Cairo just above bridge level, breaking both the sound barrier and thousands of panes of glass. A warning – a show of strength.'

'Warning?'

'Does that help you understand that this is not a game? The next time the Israelis fly over like this they could do a great deal more than break windows. Unless the Egyptians are able to protect themselves, that is. Do I make myself clear?'

For the life of him, Nick couldn't see what his role in this might be.

'And your other lie, your other sin of omission. Tell me what that was.'

He couldn't. He wouldn't. But Quinlevan appeared to know everything else. So he did. Hans's visit to the beach house at Agami. What Grace had related.

'Very well, then, dear boy. Now listen. Understand that it will be exactly like this when you deal with Hans – he and his superiors will have ways of checking. So what we have to do is give him some truth, not too damaging. Within which other information is wrapped. Inevitably they'll want to triangulate, if you get me.'

'Sorry?'

'I mean they'll want other sources to corroborate what you're passing on to them.'

'And how about Grace?'

'Your being lovers may be as coincidental as Hans running into you on the *Esperia*, or perhaps not.'

Quinlevan gave no clue as to whether this was a witticism or a hint at the truth.

'Don't worry. I'm not a judgemental Cambridge don – I deal in the practicalities of the real world.'

For the next hour they embroidered the character of the mythical communications officer in the embassy, the ostensible source of much of this information and disinformation. Nick memorised what he was to pass on.

'Next week, one of our chaps is visiting for a while. May well be that he'll come down to brief you. Good that you should have another contact anyway.' Quinlevan sounded uncharacteristically vague. 'Now, lest we forget the original, and vitally serious point of your mission, what have you got for me?'

Nick handed over his most recent sketches from the docks.

'Good. Want you to keep a close lookout for freighters. Particularly ones from Poland and the DDR. May appear civilian but still dock in the naval port. Or might be naval vessels. Send details by Morse as soon as you've got anything. Course, a few Leica snapshots would be ideal, but risks understood. That's it from me. And by the by, so glad you're comfortable with your additional role.'

Quinlevan made it sound as if he only had two roles. But Nick's kaleidoscopic view of his Alexandrian life differed: embracing Leila in the smoke-filled Reproduction Room, holding hands with Samy as they strolled through Ras-El-Tin, lying in Grace's bed at Agami, and betraying his country to Hans in the roof garden.

***

AT LUNCH IN THE Nile Hotel, after Grace had showed him her purchases, exquisitely chased little silver pillboxes and thimbles, he passed on what he'd heard about the Mirages. She listened without comment as she stirred her coffee.

Must have already known about it. Hardly likely to have overheard the news in the souk, but could have been told in the embassy, of course. Except that it had been closed and deserted. Apart from Quinlevan.

Resuming her vice-consul's wife persona when she picked up the others, Grace made good time on the desert road through great gusts of sand.

Dropping them off at his house, she whooped with surprise on noticing the front of her car. All the paint above and below the bumper and around the radiator had been sandblasted away, leaving a dull silvery metal surface.

'So you've been responsible for damage to two consular cars in two days, Dr Hellyer.'

She wagged her finger at him and drove off.

Richard and Samy departed in high spirits; with Mitri's assistance they'd negotiated a Friday slot in May at the AUC.

***

THE NEXT WEEK, NICK and Leila invigilated their examination.

At the start, Rachida slit open the sealed envelope containing the question papers she'd kept locked in the office safe.

Afterwards, he suggested to Leila that they meet at his house on Thursday to discuss and compare marks.

'Not straightforward. Better in the department.'

'But more relaxed at my place – that staffroom is appalling.'

'I know! I'll get Samy to come along as chaperone. Then it'll be all right for me to be with you – he finishes early on a Thursday afternoon.'

So Thursday 3 p.m. it was.

***

LATE ON TUESDAY AFTERNOON, Nick appeared at the DDR Cultural Centre and performed the script he'd rehearsed with Quinlevan. Hans took no notes.

'Whole place is bugged, believe me,' Quinlevan had repeated before instructing him to ask for increased payment.

Now, he did so and Hans explained that the money question had to be referred to higher authority.

'Good, good. One thing puzzles me though. Simple question, really. For what reason are you doing this? You are lecturer we know, but also friend of diplomats. Why do they tell you and afterwards you tell me these things?'

He took a deep breath and looked Hans straight in the eyes without responding.

'You need money so much? Is that what is so important to you? How can I believe what you say, if I don't know why?'

Quinlevan had prepared him for the question. So Nick trotted out the semi-truthful lines he'd learned at the embassy. Deprived childhood, teenage rebellion, Ban the Bomb, rejection of class-ridden Cambridge, desire to bring about a better world with no enmities. Sharing information, some of which he'd picked up from a bored communications officer. The only way to prevent war.

By the end, he'd almost convinced himself.

***

NICK SPENT PART OF Tuesday and Wednesday early evenings in the docks; his Morse reports were brief as he'd only spotted one new naval vessel. Quinlevan's cargo ships had not yet put in an appearance. But on the Wednesday evening something occurred that he found hard to explain. As he changed, he noticed that Samy's galabeya was not in the wardrobe.

***

ON THURSDAY AFTERNOON, LEILA and Samy arrived together bearing a heavy bag of exam scripts. Nick and Leila settled down in the sitting room to go through the marked papers and produce a list of results. Samy headed for the sunshine and placed himself in the double swing chair in the garden, stretched out like a cat, thumbing through Nick's copy of *Catch 22*.

After a while Nick went out to offer him more tea, casually mentioning the missing galabeya.

'Oh, did you visit our room on your own, Nick? I wonder what you were doing there without me.' Samy's tone was arch. 'If you really want to know, I took it home to wash. You know how dirty they get from all the sand and dust.'

Nick went back in, not knowing what to make of Samy's answer, or indeed his attitude, and tried to concentrate on the task in hand.

He and Leila worked conscientiously; soon they were down to a couple of students who, in answering his *King Lear* question, seemed to have come up with exactly the same answer.

'This happens, you know. Our students are very fluent orally but their written English isn't always as good. They memorise answers, hoping they'll fit the question. As you may know, in our culture we have a long tradition of rote-learning so it's not surprising.'

'But though these two couldn't have known what my question would be their essays are almost identical – and excellent.'

Samy drifted over, book in hand, his manner now more formal.

'We get cases like this in the Faculty Administration from time to time. I suggest you let it go.'

'But the only explanation is that they've copied. Or that the question was known and someone prepared the answer for them.'

'Don't go there, Nick, my friend. That's my advice. And, sorry, but if I'm going to get back in time for the rehearsal, I have to leave now. Okay?'

Leila looked up with a brief smile.

'Sure, Samy. See you later.'

They sat together, avoiding eye contact in the pregnant silence, only broken when he rose abruptly and told Hamid he could go home early.

After the servant's departure, he plumped himself down beside her.

'What are we going to do about it?'

Meaning the possible cheating.

'Take me upstairs now.'

Sun flooded into his bedroom and he closed the windows, but didn't touch the shutters or curtains. Always the boab to think about.

She came in from the bathroom and sat close to him on the bed. Their thighs and shoulders touched as she held his hand and took a deep breath.

'Understand me properly now. I'm engaged to Abdul and have been for a long time. He's abroad at the moment but will be back soon, and then the wedding preparations will start. There – that's something about me. What about you?'

He offered a heavily edited version of his life history.

'I know it's difficult for you, Leila, and I may have nothing to offer but trouble. But I've been so aware of you recently whenever we're in the same room. And when we held each other—'

'Yes, I've felt it too. I've only ever been with Abdul and he's the man I'm going to marry. But before that I want to make love with you.'

'Why?'

'To know what it's like to be with another man – isn't that sufficient explanation for you? Do you want me to declare undying love as well?'

His romantic illusions now thoroughly shattered, they gently undressed each other and lay between smooth cotton sheets. He stroked her firm body and kissed her cheek as she shivered under his touch. They faced each other for what seemed to be forever, Nick stiffly tense and Leila with her head buried in his chest.

'You should know that in this country it is essential that a woman is pure when she marries.'

'But Abdul?'

'No, he hasn't. No one has.'

'But—'

The distance between them grew again until she took her bag and disappeared into the bathroom. On her return, she kissed him deeply on the lips, turned away and pushed her buttocks against him.

'Take me there, please, dear Nick. This is what we do to stay a virgin. Take me now.'

And he did, gently at first and then under her moaned insistence more passionately.

Afterwards they were at peace in each other's arms and must have dozed because when they woke the sun was disappearing.

She stroked his forehead.

'Thank you. That was so wonderful. Both the sleep just now and what we did before.'

He marvelled at her directness, guessing that this moment would not come again but knowing they had to resume normality.

'You shower. I'll tidy up here.'

She disappeared while he made the bed look halfway respectable and opened the windows to dissipate the unmistakable odour of sex. Only then did he look at his watch.

He dragged on his clothes, ran downstairs, splashed his face in the downstairs toilet and tidied up the piles of exam scripts. Hearing the bell ring, he looked out to see the boab letting Samy in.

'Well, what have you two been up to in my absence, I wonder?'

Samy's left eyelid drooped into a half-wink.

'On your advice, we've decided to do nothing about the coincidence in the *King Lear* answers. Leila's going to take the marked scripts and the results into Rachida on Saturday.'

'Good decision. And on Friday?'

Samy wanting to know what he and Leila were doing on Friday? No. Hold on.

'On Friday we can spend the day in our room.'

'I like it when you say "our room".'

CHAPTER 7

A BIZARRE NORMALITY TOOK OVER and Nick found his Fridays in Ras-El-Tin surprisingly relaxing. Samy seemed to have accepted that their friendship was just that, and would not go to a physical level. Nevertheless, he conceded discreet handholding when they were out walking together.

One Friday afternoon, swirls of cigarette smoke drifted into the projection beam of a low-ceilinged cinema and peanut shells crunched underfoot as they arrived late for the start of Chaplin's *The Champion*. Tense silences were followed by roars of appreciation at Charlie's combination of bashfulness and audacity.

Other days, they sat outside a juice bar with glasses of freshly pressed sugar cane and guava, Samy chatting freely to the other customers, Nick venturing just a few words.

He returned on his own to Ras-El-Tin a couple of times each week in the afternoon or early evening. He saw no sign of the freighters but spotted a newly delivered Komar-class guided-missile patrol boat.

Sundays meant Agami with Grace and Col, accompanied by Douglas, whom Quinlevan had described as a visiting colleague.

While the major required him to stick to the truth at all times this clearly did not appear to be a reciprocal arrangement. Nick reckoned the guy was almost certainly based in Cairo.

'Douglas is as good a name as any other. No need for you to know any more about me. That way, if the balloon does go up, there's less to squeeze out of you.'

In khaki safari jacket and shorts and white knee-high cotton socks, the man looked like an off-duty South African real-estate salesman. But he was most definitely the real thing despite his youthful appearance, arriving from Cairo each weekend in an embassy car with driver.

Moreover, the information he provided had every appearance of the truth. At Agami, they went for long walks on the half-deserted beach while Douglas tested Nick on his recall of what he'd just been told. Nothing was written down.

'Planned arrival of an extra parachute-trained infantry battalion at RAF Akrotiri, Cyprus, to be based at Dhekalia. French Mediterranean fleet to start manoeuvres off the North African coast. Thought to be practising amphibious landings.'

'Why are we passing all this on to the DDR, Douglas? No one's going to attack East Germany from Cyprus, are they? Sounds a stupid question, but what's the purpose of us letting them in on it?'

'Don't know. Don't want to know. Don't need to know.'

Douglas brushed sand from his knees.

'Information. Most valuable currency of all. Of course, not always clear whether counterfeit or not.'

Post-briefing, the vice-consul and the man from the embassy strolled along to the beachside bar, while Grace and Nick made the best use they could of this brief interlude.

***

MONDAYS TO WEDNESDAYS WAS devoted to teaching. Nick found the spontaneity of his students' reactions to the characters and universal themes of Shakespearian tragedy and Dickensian fiction deeply rewarding and energising. It was as if they were considering real-life people, problems and events.

On Tuesdays, he paid his now regular visit to Hans in the DDR Cultural Centre roof garden for tea. Another acting role. He slipped into it easily, teasing the German by omitting details that he then allowed to be dragged out of him. He had no way of knowing whether Hans believed him, although on occasion the man's mask slipped, revealing momentary excitement. Hans had once mentioned the possibility of another DDR official sitting in, but dropped the idea immediately when it was met with a blank refusal.

Thursday evenings were for rehearsal, and Richard continued to drill the cast. Nick felt no real spark with Samira despite, or perhaps because of, Lucky's less than subtle encouragement.

As for Leila, no opportunity for a repetition of their afternoon together had presented itself. He would have loved to take things further, but it was she who was making the rules.

Two weeks before the first night, the company met at his house for the first dress rehearsal. English-speaking members of Lucky's extended family had been drafted in as an audience to add verisimilitude. Furniture had been shifted and piled up at one end of the sitting room to create an open space. And an improvised lighting and sound system had been rigged up.

The cast huddled in the kitchen while Samy started the introductory music.

Then the phone rang.

Nick guessed it was someone trying to reach the Amir Cinema, as his phone number was similar. He'd come to realise that if he answered with *ghalat* – wrong number – the caller would only ring back. Now, as had become his custom, he took the booking and gave an imaginary seat reservation number, thereby satisfying the caller, that is, until they reached the cinema.

But as he put down the receiver he heard an odd double click. He lifted it again and jiggled the cradle with his index finger to get a line.

No dialling tone.

Instead, he heard the music playing in the distant sitting room.

Could only be one possible explanation. But now was not the moment for investigation.

After the dress rehearsal, Mamdouh and Richard's feedback was positive. And if their consumption of large quantities of sweetmeats was anything to go by, Lucky's family had adored the evening.

As usual, Samy stayed on to help clear up after the others had left.

'Thank you very much, my friend – but best if you go now. Afraid tomorrow looks off as well.'

'Is it that Mamdouh? He was talking to you after the rehearsal, wasn't he? I saw you together, head to head. What language were you using? I can guess. I thought that Arabic was our secret. You're just like Bishop, casting me off like this.'

'No, Samy, nothing like that at all. Just telling him how pleased I was that the rehearsal had gone well. Promise. Now, I'm feeling a bit off colour. First-night nerves, I expect. Need to get my head down.'

'I could stay and look after you.'

'No, thank you.'

'But when are we going to see each other again at our place?'

'We'll have to work something out.'

'Oh. Right. It's like that, is it? See you sometime, then.'

Once on his own, Nick tried to channel his inner Scottie and formulate a rational response to his discovery.

Turn on the radio. Slowly lower the volume until only faintly audible. Close the doors. Lift the receiver in the hall for a dialling tone. Get one. Hold the cradle down.

As expected. Music playing in the sitting room. Loud and clear. Now to find the microphone. Might be easier said than done.

He returned to the sitting room. On hands and knees, he carefully examined the wires tacked to the top of the white-painted skirting board. The process was time-consuming but eventually productive. A wire, which emerged from the wall just above the skirting, ran a short distance then dived down under the floor.

Nick scrutinised the wall and was rewarded with the discovery of a pinhole in the plaster. He brought the radio over, placed it on a stool by the pinhole and further reduced the volume. Then he returned to the phone in the hall.

Clearly audible music.

He grabbed the radio and bounded up to his bedroom. Now that he knew what he was looking for, the task should be easier. An incriminating pinhole and associated wire under the head of his double bed were swiftly found. He checked using the radio in the same way, proving that the microphone was live.

The soft night air was welcoming as he sank into the garden swing chair with a whisky. The scent of jasmine mingled with darker tones from the nearby drainage channel. The trams had ceased running and cricket chirps competed with the occasional delivery lorry or taxi in the distance.

He'd had a good look at the plaster and paint around the pinholes and the bugs had clearly been there for a while. They might have been meant for his predecessor, not him, so perhaps no one had been monitoring them. On the other hand, that didn't really make any sense, as the connection to the phone line was live.

And then there was the question of exactly what had been listened to in the sitting room and bedroom.

Not so easy, that one.

Potentially, everything in the sitting room. Including the play. They must have heard all the rehearsals, and Mamdouh's script didn't beat about the bush. How on earth could the listeners have distinguished between dramatic dialogue and ordinary conversation?

He envisaged a smoky damp cellar with low-hanging neon tubes, where groups of sweating unshaven men with rolled-up shirtsleeves argued over the translation of words they were playing back over and over. It could be that transcribing the recordings from his house was providing several families with their daily bread.

Time to take stock.

Col had only spoken to him in the garden, and Grace had never come into the house. Sensible woman, as always. Samy had certainly spoken impetuously, but mainly in Ras-El-Tin, not Bulkley.

The bedroom.

Leila.

Everything she'd told him about her fiancé, everything they'd done together had been overheard. And shared with whom?

***

'WELL, HELLO, SUNSHINE.'

A rather bleary-eyed, dressing-gowned Col half-opened his apartment door the next morning.

'Do come in, though a touch early, isn't it? Party last night went on a bit. Grace still crashed out.'

'I've become interested in horticulture.'

'You what?'

'Was wondering if you could show me the consul general's rose garden.'

Col got it.

'Grab a seat. Will be with you in mo.'

After a few hours' uneasy sleep, Nick had checked the bug sites to make sure that it hadn't all been a bad dream. It hadn't. At nine, he'd taken the lift to the sixth floor of the Dafrawi Building.

He wandered across to the wide windows, drifting back to his first sight of this exciting, intimidating vista.

Col bustled in, brisk and alert now, with a jug of thick iced mango juice and two glasses.

'Yasmeen made it yesterday. Top.'

The two men made their way around to the Residence and, after Col had popped in to explain their presence to Winks, retired to the rose garden.

'Now, what's all this about, mate? Got yourself in a spot of bother, then?'

'No, or rather yes, or perhaps.'

He explained how he'd unearthed the bugs. Col praised him for his technique and then asked about distances, wires and pinhole sizes.

'Not much to do about it just now, I'm afraid. Will inform Winks at once, of course, but have to take a lead from Cairo. Just got back yesterday with the bag so no point in returning at once for a face-to-face. Tell you what though. Much better. Douglas will be here tomorrow night for your Sunday meeting. I'll bring him down to you on arrival and he can take things from there.'

Nick picked up on Col's implicit confirmation of Douglas's status.

'Go straight back home. Don't go out again – just do what you usually do. Any friends come around, make sure that conversation stays away from dangerous areas.'

***

SAMY CALLED IN THE afternoon.

'Are you feeling better, my dear? I'm really rather worried about you. And so sorry about last night. Can you forgive me? I'd love to come round and cheer you up.'

He arrived bearing grilled pigeon and rice, which they ate outdoors, a fortunate choice of location given Samy's rather malicious gossip about his Faculty Administration workmates.

Later in the evening, Nick reclined in the garden swing chair, staring up at the balance and rhythm of the night sky, sieving conversations. Yes, it was in the same chair that he'd asked for Samy's help with a place in Ras-El-Tin. Thank God. The crucial thing was that no one should get a hint of the room. Not Col, not Douglas, not even Grace, and particularly not the Egyptian authorities.

***

Douglas was nothing if not business-like when he arrived with Col.

'No point in concealing what we're doing. Now tell me how you found them.'

Nick complied.

Douglas smiled, taking a sharp spike out of a shiny metal tool case. 'First, show me the downstairs one.'

Douglas knelt down and dug around the pinhole with his spike, soon making an espresso cup-sized hole in the soft plaster. He dug deeper, reached into the hole and pulled out a dull silver aluminium cylinder the size of a large battery, attached to the wire to the skirting board.

'Ah, an old friend.'

Turning it over in his hand, he studied the red-stencilled numbers on the side.

'Yes, a B2205. Heard we supplied a consignment of these to the Egyptians a few years ago. Wondered what they'd done with them.'

Douglas carefully returned the cylinder to its hole, ensuring it didn't become detached from the wire.

'So I've been bugged by British technology, supplied through the British embassy.'

'Course these ones are seriously out of date now. Need a wired connection, you see. Now, the other one?'

Douglas carried out the same procedure in the bedroom with an identical result.

'Sit outside, shall we?' Away from prying ears, Douglas continued. 'Here's the plan. You, Nick, are not to leave this house. Egyptians now know we've found the listening devices. You pop out and they'll come and retrieve their property before we've had a chance to respond. Bugs may well have been installed to eavesdrop on the previous tenant. But they're certainly in use against you. Not making an issue of it would be a tacit admission you're up to no good. So the consul general is going to make a formal protest to the governor tomorrow.'

Col's head jerked back.

'But tomorrow's Sunday and the Consulate General is closed. Winks doesn't work on Sundays – never has. An episcopalian, you see.'

'I don't care if he's a fucking South Malayan baptist, quite frankly, Col. He'll do what I say or HMA will direct him to.'

'Douglas, who or what is HMA?'

'Sorry, Nick. Her Majesty's Ambassador.'

***

AND THUS, THE FOLLOWING day, Winks, with the demeanour of an unhappy wedding guest, shared the rear seat of the freshly cleaned and newly windscreened car with Nick, who was sporting a multi-coloured kipper tie. With a Union

Jack pennant fluttering from the car's flagstaff they arrived at the Alexandria Governorate at midday for an appointment requested on a matter of great urgency.

They climbed the honey-coloured steps of the 1950s concrete building. Two uniformed guard greeted them formally and respectfully and took them to a small side room. There they waited in silence, seated on gilded empire-style chairs. Winks picked at the sharp creases of his trousers while Nick stared blankly at the wall.

At half past twelve, an aide-cum-translator summoned them into the presence of the smoothly groomed governor.

After the usual polite formalities, the consul general explained that he had the honour of drawing the governor's attention to an incident that could be prejudicial to Anglo–Egyptian relations. Invited to proceed, he outlined the situation, emphasising that Dr Hellyer was subsidised by the British government to lecture at the university in the context of a Cultural Relations Agreement.

The governor listened sympathetically, nodding with the aide's translation. Then his manner changed and his face darkened.

'In all my years of public service to the United Arab Republic, I have never heard of such a case. Our government greatly values mutual co-operation with yours in educational and cultural spheres. I therefore find it hard to believe what you have told me, while of course accepting your word. It is, of course, possible that the listening devices you refer to were put in place by the Americans, or even the Israelis.' He paused at length. 'However, I will investigate and take appropriate action, you may be sure. I am most grateful to you for bringing the matter to my attention.'

With this he stood up, and after some bowing and hand-shaking Nick and the consul general left. On the way back, Winks loosened his tie.

'Ruddy liar, if you'll excuse my French. He was Deputy Minister for Security before taking over the Alexandria Governorate.'

The Zodiac dropped Nick off and Douglas popped into the car to receive a briefing from Winks. Then he returned to the villa and strode into the sitting room.

'Right, Nick. Let's go. We're invited to the Residence for lunch and I'd imagine that'll take at least two hours.'

Soon they were tucking into a good simulacrum of an English Sunday roast, washed down with an indifferent, slightly sour Burgundy. After the meal, and while the others took coffee in the lounge, Douglas strolled with Nick in the rose garden for the regular briefing, focusing on planned joint Anglo-French military manoeuvres.

At four, Edith's lunch guests finally left and she headed for the sanctuary of her *Telegraph* crossword book. Nick and Douglas returned to Bulkley, where they were greeted by the boab and given tea by Hamid.

When they were alone in the sitting room, Douglas got up from the sofa, put a finger to his lips and beckoned Nick over. The wall above the skirting board where the pinhole had been was smooth, and the wire had gone. The paint over the new plaster was almost dry. They went upstairs and pulled out his bed; it was the same story.

They retraced their steps – Douglas still non-verbally urging silence – and stood in the sitting room. The man from Cairo opened his metal case, took out a small electronic device and put on headphones. Frowning with concentration, he turned a knob, then moved rapidly to the centre of the room and pointed up at the ceiling. He climbed on to a dining chair and inspected the interior of the chandelier, nodded and beckoned Nick out into the garden.

'Usual story. As expected, came in when we were at lunch. Removed the old bugs. Put in a new one downstairs and, I imagine, in your bedroom as well. More modern Russian devices – use radio transmitters rather than the telephone line.'

'But Hamid and the boab were here. I don't understand.'

'Go and ask them, Nick, and see what they say.'

Both men stoutly denied that anyone had entered the house while he'd been out.

'See what I mean? Whose side do you think they're on? Not ours, that's for sure – got children or families to protect.'

'What should I do?'

'Carry on as normal. I'll see you here next weekend.'

'And the following Friday I'll be in Cairo for the play.'

'Great. I'll make sure I get a front-row seat.'

'You what?'

Douglas winked.

***

THE NEXT MORNING NICK endeavoured to speak to Leila but colleagues or students were always present. Same story on Tuesday. On the Wednesday, he finally caught her alone in a corridor but she seemed to think he was angling for a re-run of their lovemaking.

That afternoon, he identified and sketched an Osa I Fast

Attack Craft in the naval port. He sent news by Morse and the drawing to Cairo with Col the same day.

On Thursday, during the final rehearsal at his house, he grabbed a couple of minutes with Leila in the garden under the pretext of rehearsing a bit of business.

'Listen. I absolutely have to talk to you about something important. For reasons I'll explain, we can't talk about it here. When can I see you?'

'Nick, I really don't understand what this is about. What do you want? More? No. There's no reason for us to meet.'

'Yes, there is, Leila. Please trust me.'

'I'm seeing Abdul's family this weekend. Wedding discussions.'

'Can you be free next Monday afternoon, then?'

'Yes, I finish teaching at three.'

'Go to this place – it's safe.'

He gave her an envelope with the address of the room at Ras-El-Tin.

Her eyes widened.

'I can't possibly go there. No. Absolutely not.'

'You can wear a headscarf; no one will recognise you. We won't need long. I promise you that what I have to say is vital.'

'But I don't understand. Why can't you tell me now?'

'Because I can't here, not like this when we can be interrupted.'

'But that area is impossible. Don't you understand anything about this country at all? Or how things are for me?'

As if on cue, cries from the house summoned them back to the rehearsal.

'See what I mean? Come on Monday. You must. For your own sake, not mine.'

'I'll think about it.'

***

NICK'S REGULAR SUNDAY WITH the Dudleys came as a welcome relief from the agonising wait for his rendezvous with Leila.

This time they drove to El Alamein with Douglas, following the coast from Agami towards Libya. Col, in his role as Commonwealth War Graves liaison officer, gave a mini-lecture on the crucial tank battle fought there in October 1942.

'Changed the course of the war, they say, and Monty chased Rommel back all across northern Africa.'

Nick patrolled the well-tended graves of the seven thousand youthful soldiers who'd died in that campaign.

For what purpose?

He wandered further to the German war memorial, brown and fort-like. The heavy black marble slabs chronicling the names of their dead contrasted with the pure and uplifting architecture of the nearby white Italian building.

With these images at the back of his mind, he tried to concentrate on absorbing the car-park briefing from Douglas for his Tuesday encounter with Hans.

As they slid into the back seat of the car Grace ran her fingers over his thigh.

'Heard from Col about the bugs. Lucky we never did it at yours. Would have blown all their fuses.'

***

ON MONDAY, AFTER TEACHING, Nick went straight to Ras-El-Tin and informed Hassan that he was expecting a visitor.

He sat at the table, twirling a glass of tepid water, watching dust motes hanging in shafts of sunlight.

At a quarter to four, Leila finally appeared, flustered and heavily shrouded.

'This is by no means a suitable neighbourhood for a woman like me. What could have possessed you to ask me to come here?'

Her voice had a biting harshness.

He gave no response, and they sat in awkward silence at the table. To break the tension, he went down to the kitchen, and returned with glasses of tea.

Then he told her.

She stared at him as the words sunk in, her eyes boring into him.

'No. No.'

He tried to take her hand, but she shrank back and her head slumped.

Silence.

She sat up straight, pulling off the shawl and throwing it on the floor. In silence, she took her chair and jammed it under the door handle, then pointed to the bed.

'Now, my Nick, if they know as much about us as you say, then doing this cannot harm us more. Come to me.'

She undressed carefully and crept between the rough cotton sheets. Taken by complete surprise, he took a moment to follow and, in bed, was equally slow to respond.

'Come to me.'

Afterwards, she held him close for a moment before dressing.

Wrapped in her shawl, she left him alone in the dirty little room.

CHAPTER 8

LUCKY LAY MOTIONLESS ON his back, enveloped in a long coat, as Nick came on stage in the Sayed Darweesh Theatre. He knelt, facing the audience over the corpse, undid the coat belt and reached inside to investigate. There he located a hidden bag full of animal offal and intestines. He dug his hands into the bag and raised the contents towards the stage lights, like an Inca king at a ritual sacrifice.

'That's all right then. Nothing suspicious here.'

He got back to his feet ponderously, wiping his bloody hands on a large white linen handkerchief, and exited to relieved laughter.

At the British Consulate-funded post-performance party, Nick heard an imperious voice from behind him.

'Well, Dr Hellyer.'

He looked around and came face-to-face with an immaculately turned out, but still engagingly piratical Professor Naguib.

'Perhaps not what you expected to find yourself doing when you joined my department. Do come and join us, won't you?'

She gestured to a table where her husband sat alone.

'My dear, you remember Dr Hellyer. He's the new Bishop.'

'Yes, of course. You came to tea with us, didn't you?'

Before Nick could reply, Professor Naguib made one of her famous interventions.

'There are two things I wanted to mention, Dr Hellyer, apart from your performance tonight, of course. In a way, one leads on from the other.'

'Certainly, Professor.'

'I'd like to thank you for your understanding in a little matter relating to the examinations – your flexibility is much appreciated. No need to say anything more about it; my nephew keeps me informed.'

The professor continued relentlessly.

'The other thing also relates to Samy, because I want you to know that I'm so glad that you and he have become good friends. People can so easily choose the wrong companion here, as that unfortunate E.M. Forster did. What on earth could have inspired him to choose a tram driver of all people?'

'Actually, I've just been reading Forster's book about the history of Alexandria.'

A sharp clack distracted the professor's attention as boot heels were brought smartly together. A familiar voice followed.

'Professor, do forgive me for interrupting you. Can I introduce my fiancé, Captain Abdul? No, please don't stand up. Abdul has just returned from a mission overseas and I wanted you to meet him at last.'

Leila led her fiancé around the back of Nick's chair. The tall Egyptian army officer bent over to shake hands with both the professor and her husband.

'And this is my colleague, Dr Hellyer.'

Nick greeted a man in his thirties with a glow of physical fitness and a highly intelligent gaze.

'Yes, I saw you on stage – a most convincing performance, if I may say so. A born actor.'

Having thanked Abdul for his kind remarks, Nick turned to speak to Leila. But, deep in conversation with the professor, she had her back to him so he stood for a moment in silence beside the captain.

'Well, darling, you look as if you need a drink! Seen a ghost or what?'

Rescuing him, Grace took his arm and led him towards the bar.

'Large something or other for our stage star.'

Said and Ibrahim, resplendent in gold-braided uniforms, were in charge. Whisky and soda in hand, Nick followed Grace to a quieter corner of the reception, from where they could survey the guests.

'Complete waste of money, sweetie. But we had to do something to support you. Live drama in English really gets up the Frenchies' noses.'

He tried to see how a mildly subversive play translated from Arabic could be mutated into a British cultural triumph, but gave up in the attempt.

'Lunch on Sunday? Understand your friend from Cairo isn't coming this week, so no need to go out to Agami. Col and I thought of Aboukir, and maybe a boat trip. Are you on? Hope so. Now, please do introduce me to that gorgeous young playwright.'

Nick accepted the invitation and took Grace across the room to meet Mamdouh, who was immensely flattered by her attention and not at all offended by her halting Arabic.

***

THE NEXT MORNING, HE was up early and at the Faculty with his bag before nine; they were all going in Lucky's father's venerable Packard and the capacious boot was crammed with costumes and props.

Lucky gunned the engine of the huge American car as they set off, with Richard and Nick in the front and the other five crushed together in the back.

Lucky dropped Nick off first, at the Nile Hotel, then drove the others out to the Heliopolis suburb, where they were staying with friends.

Prior to his meeting with Douglas, he plunged into the network of small streets behind the Mogama Building to buy offal for the evening's performance. Then, armed with a straw shopping bag concealing his newspaper-wrapped haul, he hurried to the embassy. Sweating in the hot sun, he waited for a guard to take him to reception.

'Food in that, sir? Can't take it in with you, I'm afraid.'

The guard took the bag and placed it carefully outside the entrance door.

In the secure room, Douglas waited in a state of some excitement.

'All worked out rather well your being here this weekend. Lots to go over – whole operation turning into something rather super high priority. Good that we're not on a beach or in a car park. Never very sure how safe those venues actually are.'

They sat on hard chairs at one end of a stained pine conference table, half-facing each other. Douglas's hands rested lightly on a thick buff official-looking folder.

'As you can see, quite a bit of traffic for you, so let's get going.'

'Wouldn't it be easier just to let me read the messages?'

'I can see where you're coming from, Nick. But this way fixes the information in your auditory memory, believe me.'

Nick concentrated hard as Douglas read the messages to him, listening, memorising, mentally filing. It was a craft he'd come to enjoy, a skill he was still developing, almost to the extent of not processing the content of what he heard. However, on this occasion astonishment must have shown on his face because Douglas called an immediate halt.

'We're about halfway through and I know there's a lot for you to take on board. Do you want a break?'

Nick nodded. He slumped, elbows on the table, head in hands, trying to work out the logic behind what he was being told.

'Shall I go on, now?'

'I don't think I can take in any more until I've got some kind of handle on what you're asking me to relay.'

'How do you mean?'

'It's the exact opposite of what I've been told to pass on so far. How could I possibly have any credibility left with Hans? Now there aren't going to be any Anglo–French naval manoeuvres? Now the practice amphibious landings in Tunisia have been cancelled? Now the parachute battalion in Cyprus is returning to RAF Lyneham?'

He paused.

'I always understood there would be disinformation mixed in, but now it would appear that *all* my past information was misleading.'

Douglas regarded him carefully.

'We do understand that this is your first time in the field.'

'No need to patronise me.'

'Listen. I'm well aware that you weren't trained as a double agent. Vital thing to appreciate is that you're merely a conduit. You need to believe in what you're telling them, so that they, in turn, believe you. But to do that successfully, you can't, and mustn't, analyse the intelligence.'

'So you lot make no distinction between truth and lies?'

'Us lot? You've had no problems, so I've been told, in leading a double life in Alexandria.'

Before he could wonder which particular double life was being referred to, Douglas ploughed on.

'What is truth anyway? Not for you or me to speculate on the truth of anything you've already told them, or are going to tell them. That's for others to deal with – we're just the operators, the foot soldiers.'

'Really? Really? You say that from the cosy security of your diplomatic status – it's my neck on the line, not yours.'

'Precisely.'

Nick was afraid that Douglas would carefully put the tips of his fingers together and incline his head back, in which case he would have no option but to thump him.

'That's exactly the point. That's why you're so valuable to us. Can't tell you how valuable because I don't know. Can assure you that all this secure-room malarkey ain't exactly routine. Time for you to get it – the key thing is that you're deniable.'

'Deniable?'

'Exactly.'

'Deniable?'

'You don't work for us and never have worked for us. This is what we would put out if you were rumbled. A rogue, a loose cannon – choose your cliché. Don't expect us to come running to your rescue. We'll hang you out to dry and walk away.'

'Oh, yeah?'

'Sure. The whole point about information is that it depends on how it's evaluated – and the source is very important in that process. Otherwise, we could just take out advertisements in the *Egyptian Gazette*.'

'Sorry, Douglas. Got to go. Quickly. Where's the—?'

Douglas pressed a button and one of the uniformed men escorted him to a toilet.

So this was what shit-scared meant. He tried to immerse his burning face in cold water, but the basin was too small.

He resumed his briefing, and both men were surprised by the accuracy of his recollection.

British reconnaissance flights along the Lebanese coast from Cyprus had been cancelled and two Oberon-class submarines that had been on patrol outside Egyptian waters had been recalled to Devonport. French paratroops, which had been expected in Algiers, remained in France and the main French Mediterranean fleet was sailing towards Marseilles. The US spy ship *Liberty* had taken up station in the eastern Mediterranean.

When tested towards the end of the session, he passed with flying colours.

'That's the spirit, Nick. Believe in it all, and sound not just convincing, but convinced. Now – some supplementary details. They're bound to have follow-up questions, so here's some stuff you can reluctantly divulge under questioning.'

Nick packed all this additional information into another compartment in his head.

'London would love to have some photos, you know. You gave them nothing this week, so don't forget the day job.'

'I won't.'

Douglas sent him on his way with an open-palmed slap on the back and he exited the embassy gates with his shopping bag.

***

WHILE THE THEATRE IN Alexandria had contained university staff and others whom they knew, the Cairo audience in the Falaki Theatre was an unknown quantity. Mamdouh had been hopeful of a few critics and Richard sure of a good student crowd, but in the event it was a sell-out.

Nick dashed on stage, almost tripping over the corpse, knelt, faced the audience, and dug into the hidden bag. He held up a double handful of intestines and stared blankly out into the lights until he became acutely aware of something wriggling against his palms. The offal, still warm from its hours in the sun, was seething with hundreds of white maggots.

Coughing and spluttering announced that the stink had reached the front rows. The clatter of seats as some ran for the exits, handkerchiefs over their mouths, was rapidly eclipsed by laughter and applause when the curtain came down.

Nick and Lucky rushed to wash off the stench, while the rest of the cast performed the final act.

'*Mish maoul, jani.*'

Lucky was in the next shower cubicle.

'Unbelievable, I mean. How could you do that? *Magnoon helas!* Completely crazy!'

Nick had hoped for time alone with Leila after the show, but she and Samy had left immediately for the last train to Alexandria. Instead, he invited Lucky, Sohail and Samira back to the rooftop bar of the Nile Hotel, where Lucky insisted on paying for large rum and colas. Dance music filtered up from the disco on the floor below. The sisters tolerated Lucky's enthusiastic boisterousness, although they hardly touched their own drinks.

'Come on, let's boogie.'

Lucky pulled Sohail to her feet.

'Why don't you two come as well? Don't know what you'd get up to if you were left here on your own!'

Samira shook her head.

As they sat together, looking out at the lights of the Cairo night sky, she turned her deep-brown eyes to him.

'You were great tonight, you know. But you must be aware that Lucky's trying to throw us together – and, to be frank, I neither need it or like it. However, that doesn't mean that we can't decide to be friends, does it?'

Emboldened by her candour, he took her arm and they walked down to the disco. Lucky and Sohail were in the middle of the circular dance floor and the revolving spotlights caught Lucky's gleaming teeth as he held out his arms.

The four of them joined hands, dancing in a ring, picking up speed in time with the music. The rhythmic movement and the damp warmth of Samira's clasp excited Nick. Lucky pulled the whole circle around, moving with joy and abandon, sweating profusely despite the air-conditioning, then dropped on to his right knee.

'Don't worry about me. Just need to pause for a moment.'

Lucky's eyes closed as the others gathered around him. Sohail turned to Nick.

'Help me. It's not the first time.'

They got Lucky back to his feet but he immediately lurched towards one of the banquettes lining the walls. Sohail was decisive.

'Not here. Your room, Nick?'

Together they got Lucky upstairs and into bed. Nick and Samira went out on to the balcony, leaving Sohail alone with her husband.

'I wish he wouldn't drink so much. My sister worries a lot about him. He always seems outgoing and sunny, but—'

'I'm not sure if this is what you're getting at, but he's told me one or two things about his role with the family estate.'

'Exactly. He's frustrated by spending his time running it rather than living his own life.'

'But why can't he?'

'Well, his parents aren't getting any younger and he's their only son.'

Nick was touched, not only by Samira's concern for her brother-in-law, but also by the fact that she'd confided in him. They stood side by side and he put his arm around her shoulder.

'I'm sure he'll be fine.'

She nestled into him quietly and when, a little later, they went back into the bedroom Lucky was sitting up. Sohail gave them a weak smile.

'He's feeling a bit better so I think we can go now.'

Nick went down with them and helped Lucky into the back seat of a taxi, where he half-lay with head thrown back and mouth open. Sohail got in beside him.

'We'll call for you here at midday tomorrow – that'll give him time to rest. And thank you for all your help, Nick.'

'Oh, my bag!'

Samira jumped out of the taxi.

'It's still in your room.'

'I can get it for you.'

'No, that's not necessary. Sohail, you and Lucky go on. I'll follow you in a minute.'

'Are you sure? We can wait for you. Get the bag – be quick and then we can leave together.'

'No, really. Take Lucky back now and I'll catch up with you.'

'Then, yes, if that's all right with you. See you soon, sister.'

Nick and Samira watched the taxi leave and took the lift. Once in his darkened room they held each other wordlessly, then wandered out on to the balcony again. He stroked her long dark hair, feeling growing desire but not wanting to offend or frighten her. They stood for a long time until finally her fingers entwined themselves with his, and one very gentle kiss followed another.

'Samira?'

No reply.

They moved together into the dark room, then naked into bed. She held him tight and he could just make out her face in the gloom.

But his arousal had mysteriously vanished and Samira was left with a limp relic of it in her hand.

'I'm so sorry. I don't know why. Let me—'

'Is it me? Don't you want me? Aren't I good enough for you?'

'No, no, you're wonderful, and I want you so much, it's just that—'

'Just what? That I'm not Leila?'

'I don't know what you mean.'

'Oh, don't you?'

She swung her legs out of the bed and pulled on her clothes.

'Or perhaps you'd prefer Samy. That's what they say about you.'

'Samira—'

She left with her bag, closing the door softly behind her as he lay in the darkness, wondering how it had all gone so horribly wrong.

He dozed intermittently until dawn, then finally fell deeply asleep.

***

GRATEFUL FOR A LATE start, he shifted uneasily from foot to foot outside the Nile Hotel at noon. Finally, the Packard pulled up with a loud blast of the horn and an ebullient Lucky at the wheel.

'Jump in, my friend. Can't hang around all day.'

Mamdouh, Richard and Samira were in the back, so Nick joined a relieved Sohail on the front bench seat.

'He's almost himself again, as you can see.'

Lucky headed for the desert road as the back-seat trio analysed and gloried in the previous night's performance. Halfway across the desert they stopped for lunch at a rest house, then Sohail took over at the wheel. Soon Lucky fell asleep with his head on Nick's shoulder.

'Hey, sister …' They were passing Lake Mariout at the entrance to Alexandria. '… my turn now!'

'But Samira, you don't—'

'Don't what? You promised me I could last night! Now let me drive!'

'That was then and this is now – I wasn't thinking straight.'

But Sohail pulled over and Samira leapt out.

'I'm in charge now. Budge over, sister. And you – you get in the back seat.'

Nick did as he was instructed and Samira took the wheel, weaving the big car in and out of donkey carts, hand-barrows, rickety open lorries, petrol tankers, private cars, yellow and black taxis, cyclists, motorcyclists and the ubiquitous buses belching diesel fumes in their wake.

On a straight stretch of Al-Horreya, as it passed the Sporting Club, she picked up a little speed. Dusk was descending rapidly and crowds struggled to clamber on to buses.

A man rushed for the gates of the club. He dodged between a taxi and an over-laden motorcycle, and looked the wrong way before running straight into Samira's path. She braked hard and swerved but there was a thud as the Packard hit him. As the car slowed, Nick looked back to see the man lying in the road, people streaming towards him.

Then he heard Lucky's commanding voice, all sleep gone. 'Drive on for a hundred metres and pull in.'

Samira, head down, did as she was told. Lucky got out and walked steadily back to the crowd. It parted to let him through, then enveloped him. Although some pedestrians took notice of the Packard, the bustle of evening traffic filled the road.

Nick sat in impotent silence in the rear. The darkness became complete.

A loud rap on the car bodywork. Lucky.

'Let's go.'

'How can we leave? How is he? Is an ambulance coming?'

'Calm down, Nick. Nothing for you to be concerned about. A broken leg, I think. I gave him sixty pounds – enough to live on while it mends.'

'What about the police?'

'Listen, my friend, not everything is as it seems. My precious sister-in-law doesn't actually have a driving licence, so the last thing we need is for the police to be involved. Anyway, he was clearly a poor man so that was quite a lot of money for him. In the long run, he'll be happy with the way things turned out.'

'Don't you care at all? We should take him to hospital.'

Samira smashed her hand against the steering wheel. 'You have no right to get high and mighty and moralistic, Dr Hellyer.'

'What do you mean?'

'After you tried to rape me in the hotel last night.'

Lucky gaped.

'Samira, what happened?'

'You know, he came on strong to me. Forced me into bed.'

'Nick. Is this true? Did you?'

'Well – yes and no, I suppose. But I didn't—'

'How could you?'

'Truth be told, you encouraged me to get close to her.'

'As friends, yes.' Lucky glanced at his wife. 'But not like that. Big misunderstanding.'

'Don't worry, Lucky. Nothing happened. When it came to the crunch he couldn't get it up – seems the rumours are true and he prefers boys, like Bishop.'

'She *was* willing. You must believe me.'

Lucky jumped out and pulled open the rear door.

'I'm afraid you'd better go Nick. Now. I'm sorry but I'll not have you first assault Samira and then insult her. Get out and goodnight.'

The others turned their heads away. Nick retrieved his bag and slunk away as the Packard sped off.

His path took him past the accident scene. The victim, partly covered with a sack, had been moved to the side of the road and was surrounded by a chattering crowd of the curious, the morbid, and those sensing an opportunity. A camera flash lit up the man's unshaven face and bloodied thigh. Nick kept his head down and trudged steadily on.

CHAPTER 9

'You're in the paper! Show him, Col!'

Grace pulled out into the traffic and headed for Aboukir.

'Not exactly front-page news but you're there!'

Flicking through Sunday's *Egyptian Gazette,* dreading an account of a hit-and-run accident outside the Sporting Club, Nick was relieved to come across the review: *Gutsy performance steals show.*

'Congratulations, sunshine. Always knew you had it in you, mind.'

He stared out of the side window as they sped past San Stefano. While he loved this magical city, he would always be alien to it. He was 'other', a water-skater beetle, at ease with the surface but not penetrating it.

They skirted the park and palace of Montazah and the beach at Marmoura, then headed down the dusty road to Aboukir. Grace's hair thrashed about in the gusts from the open window.

Their destination was a low white building at a point where the road met the beach. Outside stood weather-beaten wooden tables and decrepit upright wicker chairs. White paper tablecloths, held down by stones, fluttered in the breeze.

Col pointed out over the bay.

'Peaceful now, isn't it? Course, all very different two hundred and fifty years ago. Then you had Napoleon's army shooting bits off the Sphinx, and Nelson defeating the French fleet in this very bay.'

'Here?'

'Yep, over two thousand French and several hundred British sailors died. Called the Battle of the Nile, but in fact took place right in front of where your good selves are now sitting.'

The first customers at the beach café, they were soon seated in front of a shimmering tray of raw halved sea urchins and finger-like goose barnacles on a bed of dark-green seaweed. Grace squealed as Col passed her the seafood.

'Those ones look like little boys' willies and the sea urchins are all spiky!'

'You're wrong, Grace. Goose barnacles can reproduce without having sex.'

'Wouldn't want to know about that, Nick, thank you. And I'm not eating them – they're all yours, boys.'

Grace patrolled the shoreline, picking up and discarding pebbles until a wonderful aroma of fennel marked the arrival of grilled sea bass and a tray piled high with fried potatoes.

'Ah! Fish and chips! Heaven!'

As they were having coffee, a thin man in a short frayed grey galabeya approached the table. Bent with age and patchily shaven, he spoke slowly and very carefully in English.

'*A* seahorse, *a* lovely seahorse.'

Grace gave him five piastres for the dried seahorse, but refused to buy further ones which he produced from an old cotton shoulder bag.

'Must have learnt his English during the war.'

'Yes, Grace. But which war? Was there ever a time when we weren't fighting in, or occupying Egypt?'

Col spluttered, spilling coffee on to the sand.

'Not recently, mate, no. But in a way, you may be right because, believe it or not, in 1882 the British navy actually bombarded Alexandria for ten hours.'

A tanned man in shorts, who'd been perched on the side of a battered white sailing boat, approached the table.

'Trip to Nelson's Island? Very safe. *Khamsa gnee*, only five pounds.'

He smiled engagingly at Grace, who grinned back.

'Oh, yes, let's. Just need to go to the little girls' room first.'

The small boat was soon pitching, rolling and occasionally ducking into the swell. Nick felt a little queasy and noticed Col holding on tightly to the side. Grace, seemingly unaffected, turned from chatting to the boatman.

'Mustafa used to work as a pilot on the Suez Canal.'

Presumably that had been before Nasser had nationalised it in 1956, triggering the attack by the Israelis, French and, yet again, the British.

Soon they came into the lee of the island.

'There we are, my friends. Very smooth here. You want to go on land? Or have a beer or a smoke?'

The boat rocked as Col got to his feet and stretched out his arms over his head.

'Not sure. Wouldn't mind a stroll on the island myself. And a beer sounds good too. But none of us smoke.'

Mustafa pulled out a small white plastic cool chest from under a seat, then opened and handed Col a chilled Stella. He skilfully rowed the boat into the sharply shelving beach. The vice-consul pulled on a sun hat and, clutching his beer, strode off across the island. Then the boatman moved to smooth water ten metres from the shore and anchored.

With an unsettlingly wolfish grin, Mustafa squatted down in the centre of the boat and, reaching between his knees, loosened a couple of boards. He fished underneath with one hand and came out with two long red rubber tubes with mouthpieces, a glass bowl and a metal tray the size of an ashtray. Constructed, they created a perfectly serviceable small hookah. With an air of triumph, he peeled back the aluminium foil from a golf-ball-sized package and held the contents aloft.

'Smoke?'

'Well, that rather changes things, doesn't it? Are you game, Nick?'

'*Khamsa gnee*, five pounds for two.'

'You'll join me, Nick, won't you? It'll help.'

'Go on then.'

They settled down side by side on the boards, rough white cotton cushions supporting their heads against the side of the boat, knees in the air. Mustafa got the hookah going efficiently and soon each intake of breath through the brownish fake-ivory mouthpieces produced a stream of bubbles through the water in the bowl.

The sunshine, the rocking of the boat, Grace's proximity and the power of the dope melded into a single sensation. Mustafa had retreated to the stern and was dangling his right hand in the water, staring away from them across the bay.

He felt Grace slip her hand into his and took in a dreamy smile through half-closed eyes.

'It's been years. So good.'

He squeezed her hand and surrendered to the warmth of the sun on his eyelids, the hardness of the boards and the splashing of wavelets against the hull.

He wasn't aware of having drifted off, but must have. When he surfaced slowly he realised he was inhaling only air from the hookah.

Mustafa was standing over them, smiling.

'More?'

Grace's mouthpiece lay on the boards beside her.

'God knows how strong that was. Once is enough, thank you.'

As Mustafa got on with cleaning and dismantling the hookah, Grace, to conceal herself from the shore, snuggled up low to Nick.

'You are something else, you know.'

With her forefinger, she made rings in the hair on the side of his head.

'If Col and I weren't such an item, I might just be tempted to jump ship. But got to think about the boys – and, of course, the bloody office.'

She lapsed into a silence that he had absolutely no desire to break. Her speed and brilliance of mind were dazzling, yet she was so hard to pin down. He saw himself again as a four-teen-year-old trying to catch a sparrow that had flown into his room. Whenever he'd approached, clutching a tea towel, it had fluttered effortlessly on to the top of another high cupboard.

But the longer he lay glancing sideways at her serene face the more it seemed that he himself was the nervous creature, disorientated and vulnerable.

What 'bloody office'? By her own account, Grace had little to do with the consulate apart from going to parties and entertaining. But maybe she was more, much more, than the diplomatic wife she portrayed herself to be.

Equally, the idea of setting up home somewhere with a Col-less Grace, but with their two kids, was hard to take on board.

Nick's doped mind span these candyfloss permutations as they lay together, her head on his shoulder.

'Going out to Agami tomorrow.'

'Can't come, darling. You know I teach on Mondays.'

'Not what I meant at all – you'd be *de trop*, sweetie. I'm entertaining your friend Hansie, you see.'

'No, I don't see.'

'It's for your sake, sweetheart. All for you really. I shall lie back and think of Hellyer.'

'Why?'

'Triangulation. Like a threesome, you know. Not really! I only give him a bit so he believes what you tell him. Don't let it worry you – a gal's gotta do what a gal's gotta do. Did you ever see Doris Day in *Calamity Jane*?'

He'd felt no guilt about deceiving Col but the thought of her in bed with Hans drove him wild. He ripped his hand away and smashed his fist into the side of the boat, making a startled Mustafa jump.

'Okay, mister? No problem, no? Sometimes it works bad, the hashish. You want lie down? Are you okay, miss? You want lie down too?'

'Oh, I see! You want to fuck her as well, do you? Right, you go ahead – I'm going to have a dip.'

He stood unsteadily, then half-jumped, half-fell over the side into the surprisingly deep water. Weighed down by his clothes, at first he went straight under but made it to the beach in a clumsy dog paddle.

It was there, on the flotsam-strewn sand, that fifteen minutes later Col found him seated, head resting on drawn-up knees, shivering in the hot sun.

'Hey, all right, squire? Been for a swim in your clothes, then?'

The vice-consul signalled for Mustafa to bring the boat in to shore.

'Interesting place this. You should've come with me – found what looked like graves.'

Nick's clothes dried out as the boat swept them through the choppy water back to Aboukir. He felt slightly queasy, but most of all deeply ashamed. Mustafa hadn't turned a hair at the incident and had helped him and Col back with skill and a smile. Grace had withdrawn into herself; eyes fixed on the flapping of the sail, she trailed her left hand in the water.

The nausea hit him when they were back on dry land. Stumbling, he ran towards the toilet and almost made it; he threw up on the sand. A glass of lukewarm water later, he was in the back seat with his head out of the open window, trying to keep the remaining contents of his stomach in place.

'Going to be all right?'

Col helped him out of the car on arrival.

'Glad we're leaving you in Hamid's hands. Call if there's

anything we can do. Must confess, don't feel too bright myself.'

Nick spent the next few hours in the bathroom, poised between the toilet and the hand basin. Hamid stayed late and left him propped up in bed with a jug of cold water and a plate of dry bread.

He slept fitfully, drifting in and out of consciousness, either sweating profusely or shivering.

***

THE NEXT MORNING, HAMID came early, bringing him life-saving sweet tea. It gave him strength to phone Rachida and cancel his lectures for the day. He was genuinely surprised by, and taken with, her concern for him.

'We do get summer sicknesses here – it's a little early for them, but perhaps that's what you have.'

It was only later that he learnt that 'summer sickness' was a local euphemism for cholera.

By midday, he was sitting out in the garden. Hamid called him to the phone.

'How are you, darling?'

He filled in Grace tersely.

'Thought I'd call before leaving for Agami. I'm fine. Col's got the same as you – spent the night on the toilet and finally slept in the bath. Take care, won't you, lover? You're very precious, you know.'

'Drive safely.'

'Yes, darling. I'll take every precaution.'

The dope could be ruled out, then, because she was well. As could seasickness. The finger of suspicion moved to the goose barnacles and sea urchins.

Hamid brought him some chicken broth with rice and a jug of homemade lemon cordial. He ate, drank, dozed and mused the afternoon and evening away.

Early to bed, he nevertheless mentally ran through the Cairo briefing from Douglas again, visualising how he'd pass the information on to Hans.

***

THE NEXT DAY, RACHIDA was sweetness incarnate when he arrived at the department.

'Oh, you look so pale, Dr Hellyer. Our climate is not the best for you delicate Englishmen, you know. I really think you should go home and rest now.'

While he wouldn't have minded taking her advice, he got through his classes and took the tram to Ramleh Station. The walk to the DDR Cultural Centre cleared his mind, and he felt more in control of himself when Hans greeted him in the roof garden. He blotted out visions of his host and Grace in bed together and, once they were seated, set out to deceive him.

'So, my friend, I congratulate you on your great success in the theatre. Therefore, I wonder if you are thinking perhaps of resigning from your academic and other activities and instead concentrating on the drama.'

This had to be a joke, although the German sounded sincere and earnest.

'And what do you have for me today, please?'

As Nick recited the first part of his brief, Hans's facial expression – self-avowed expert poker player that he was – changed. His earlier bonhomie was replaced by an incipient smirk, while his responses became monosyllabic as he checked that he understood correctly.

'And.'

'Again?'

'So?'

'Back?'

'Stop.'

Hans got up, crossed the garden and went indoors, leaving Nick in the shady warmth, looking out over the rooftops. He resolutely pushed thoughts of Grace away, concentrating on those compartments of his mind that he'd filled in Cairo.

'Please to continue.'

As Nick resumed, Hans listened carefully and correctly as always, sitting upright in his chair. Now, though, despite the straight face, he revealed little quivers of excitement as he urged Nick on.

'Is that all? No more? Very well. It is enough. More than enough.'

Hans disappeared again; he returned five minutes later with an erect man in his fifties with silver-rimmed glasses, a brown crew cut and long, pointed, dandyish shoes.

'Here is my colleague.' He introduced the stranger with a wave of his arm, but gave no name.

'Sorry, Hans. We agreed only you.'

'Listen, Herr Dr, you will do what I ask now. Or, how do you say, I will throw you at the wolves.' Hans thrust his head back and gave a barking laugh. 'A traditional English expression, I understand. I am sure you are familiar with it. Now please you will carefully answer my colleague's questions.'

The man with the crew cut took him forwards and backwards over what he'd just told Hans, not concealing for a moment the evident fact that their conversation had been bugged.

Nick allowed his questioner to extract the supplementary information furnished by Douglas little by little. Eventually the colleague withdrew, followed by Hans, who returned ten minutes later in an expansive mood.

'Well, my friend, thank you. Discussion with Berlin will of course be needed. But my colleague thinks it may be appropriate to take our relationship with you to a new level.'

Nick hid his sweaty palms under his thighs.

'That's all I can say now. If you'd like to come with me, I can pass on to you our usual expression of gratitude.'

***

As Nick walked down Saad Zaghloul in search of a taxi, he yearned for his bed. However, on adding the dollars to the envelope in his top desk drawer, his hand touched the Leica and he recalled Douglas's words. He pulled the camera and three films out, stuffed them in his jacket pocket and headed for Ras-El-Tin.

Hassan greeting him warmly but when Nick opened the wardrobe door to change, his head swam. Fear of being followed, fear of being caught, fear of this being the night when it all ended engulfed him.

Soft chatter from the narrow street outside filtered through the shutters, and shafts of sunlight played on his legs as he stretched out on the bed.

He dozed – to images of the sparkling sea at Aboukir and the cheerful bubbling sound of the hookah.

The cries of pedlars and the screams and laughter of children called in to supper eventually awoke him as the street came alive with the advent of darkness.

He closed his eyes again, half-aware of footsteps, snatches of conversations, distant lorries, and dogs.

But then, something closer. Much closer.

Someone breathing shallowly. Someone moving on tiptoes. Someone bringing danger.

Scottie had taught him that surprise and patience were the keys. Be patient and then surprise them. Minimum force. Go for the windpipe for silence. Not too hard, of course – you might want to question them later.

He detected a fragrance that he half-recognised and felt the warmth of a body. Through quarter-open lashes he made out the silhouette of a short figure standing poised over him.

His patience lasted only a few seconds before he acted. He swung around off the bed, his legs scything through the air, catching the man at the knees and knocking him to the floor. The intruder gave out a high-pitched cry as Nick landed on his chest. As his hands fastened around the man's neck, the body underneath him writhed and tossed before going limp.

Mindful of Scottie's advice, he relaxed his grip. At once he received a bony knee in the groin, knocking him sideways. Inflamed by the pain, he swung his right fist wildly, connected with his assailant's face and heard the crack of the impact as the head hit the floor. He disentangled himself carefully; he wouldn't be fooled again. As his eyes adjusted to the darkness, the identity of the white-shirted figure lying beneath him became shockingly clear.

Moving over to the door, he snapped on the single bare light bulb to reveal Samy rising to his knees, one hand to his face and tears in his eyes.

'Why did you do that?'

'I didn't know it was you.'

'How could you be so violent?'

'I was afraid.'

'Help me up.'

'Yes, my friend, of course. I truly didn't know it was you.'

Nick stretched out his right hand and Samy pulled himself up. Nick put his arm around the Egyptian's shoulders in apology.

'No, don't touch me.'

Samy spun out of his grasp, backed off, then charged wildly, head down, straight into his midriff. Propelled backwards, Nick lost his footing and cracked his head hard on the edge of the table. Samy dragged him, half-stunned, up into a chair, whipped out a coil of rope from a bag on the floor and quickly wound it around his upper body. Nick tried to resist by kicking out, but Samy punched him twice in the stomach before completing his rope work.

'You bastard! You hurt me! You deceived me!'

Samy prowled around the room with an angry swagger.

'Very smart, aren't you, Mr Clever? Well, I'm not so stupid either, you know. This is *our* place, isn't it?'

Nick nodded. 'No one else knows about it.'

'Yes, they do, Mr Clever, Dr Clever, Professor Clever. *I* know you brought Leila here.'

Nick sat passively, giving Samy his full attention and trying to read his body language. He sensed a contradiction; while the words were wild, the body was lithe, tense and well under control.

'I was yours. You could have had me, and I wanted so much for you to have me. But you went with her, brought her to our place, and had her instead. Here. I know.'

'How?'

Samy's voice swung wildly from a vicious deep hiss to a falsetto.

'How do you think? Hassan told me. A visit from a woman on her own in this area is something special. He listened outside the door and gave a detailed description of what he'd heard. Well, what's all this with a girl's arse anyway? You could have had mine. I'm sure Abdul will be extremely interested in what I have to tell him about you and his intended.'

'Let me go, Samy, and we can talk things through. It can all be fine again – you'll see. You and I understand each other – she's just a woman, but I'm your true friend. You know that.'

'Okay, I'll release you, Mr Clever Dick. But first of all, I'm going to release your dick and then I'm going to cut it off.'

Samy pushed the chair around. He unbuckled Nick's belt and pulled his trousers down to the ankles. The Egyptian stood and looked at him for a moment, smiled triumphantly, then knelt down and yanked at his pants, a knife clasped in his right hand.

'Come on, let's see you!'

Nick brought his right leg up, catching Samy hard on the chest and then on his left cheek, knocking him back on to the floor. Nick staggered to his feet and spun around, the chair still behind him, as Samy, knife in hand, tried to scramble off the floor. The chair caught Samy hard on the temple and he went down with a crash, shaking the floorboards. He lay motionless as dust filled the air.

Silence. Just Nick's own frantic panting.

Hassan would have heard both the shouts and the fight. Moving as quickly as he could with his trousers around his ankles and the chair tied to his back, he shuffled to the door.

'*Ta'aalla hina!* Come here!'

Hassan came running suspiciously quickly and stood in the doorway, shaking his head and wringing his hands, unwilling to venture in. The landlord's eyes took in Samy on the floor, knife still in hand, and Nick, half-naked, bound to the chair.

Hassan took the knife and cut the ropes, saying nothing, snatching backward glances at Samy.

Nick pulled his trousers up, rummaged in his right-hand pocket for his wallet and gave Hassan ten pounds. He dashed down the stairs, leaving Hassan bending over Samy.

Threatening pools of blackness in the now quiet street hit him as he ran out of the building. He moved at a steady pace as he'd been taught, from light to light, head down, occasionally glancing from side to side, to seek cover.

Two youthful dark-clad figures burst from an alley and wrestled him to the ground. One landed with his knees on Nick's shoulders and pummelled his face with his fists; the other rifled through his trouser pockets.

Nick lay quiescent for a moment, feeling his keys and coins go and hands pull at his wristwatch. They could have those, but not the wallet and camera in his jacket. He twisted abruptly, unseating the boy on his shoulders and punching him as he fell. He scrambled to his feet, caught the other teenager with two hard kicks to the lower body, then turned and sprinted off. Exhilaration was soon tempered by realism as he heard the pounding of feet behind him.

A couple of minutes later, he slowed to a halt, lungs burning, any illusion that he could outrun his attackers quashed.

He glimpsed the flashing blue-and-red sign of the Spitfire Bar. He'd been there with Richard, remembered a warm seamen's drinking hole with music. Shelter from the storm.

Bagging the only vacant table, close to a tiny stage, he ordered a large whisky and water and struggled to get his breath back.

Samy was going to peach on him to Abdul, wasn't he? He'd said so. And he would. No doubt. The fight would only have strengthened the Egyptian's resolve. Nick had seriously underestimated the importance Samy had attached to their relationship. Indeed, things might be even worse if his conjectures about Samy playing a double game turned out to be correct.

A tall wiry guy in a leather jacket occupied the stage beside him. A record landed on the turntable, pulsating Arab music filled the room and coloured lights over the stage started flashing. Though two tables were filled with partying Egyptian men distinguished by sharp suits and haircuts, the majority were occupied by the gypsies of the ocean, merchant seamen from every continent.

The lights dimmed and a woman with a long diaphanous black skirt and an imperious expression appeared. She held her hand behind her neck and, to increasingly fevered cries, began a slow belly dance. The rhythm of the drums built and the swivel of her hips matched the tempo. The spectacle was more trance-like than erotic as the irresistible thump-thump of the drums combined with the thick heat of the crowded room. Sailors surrounded the stage and as the dance reached its climax the lights flashed faster. Wild applause followed, but when the crowd moved in on the dancer Leather Jacket intervened.

The seamen slowly dispersed, all except one. About sixty, short and bald, in a blue uniform shirt with epaulettes, he possessed an air of energy and authority.

'So sweet! Dance for me only.'

He pulled out a handful of dollar bills, stuffing them into the dancer's cleavage. She glanced at Leather Jacket, who retrieved the money to some applause.

'Okay, one dance.'

The short man stood alone on the stage in front of her, transfixed, backed by a ring of sailors. When the dance had concluded and the dancer and her minder had left, he remained, staring out into the lights.

Finally, with delicate precision, he bent to his knees, leaned forward, stood on his head and put his thumbs in his ears. Then he waggled his fingers and stuck out his tongue.

Upside down, he locked eyes with Nick, who grinned nervously and clapped too loudly. The short man flipped back on to his feet with surprising dexterity and came up to him with a broad smile.

'Captain Jan de Herdt of Antwerp, at your service.' The captain doffed an imaginary cap and bowed. 'I have seen you sitting alone, so please to come and join us.'

'Why not?' Nick smiled and introduced himself.

The captain steered him to the back of the room, explaining that he and his crew had just delivered a tugboat to the Egyptian Navy and were leaving for Belgium early in the morning.

'But first we party!' Captain de Herdt gestured towards a bottle-strewn table with half a dozen seamen slumped around it. 'My crew. And my boss.'

His finger moved to a smaller table where a man with cropped grey hair sat with his back to the room.

'This is Nick, my new friend.'

The crew had responded to Nick's arrival with a not unfriendly, slightly ironic round of applause, but the grey-haired man only gave a bleak smile as he glanced back over his shoulder.

'We have already met.'

CHAPTER 10

'OLD FRIENDS? THAT IS good.'
The tugboat captain raised his glass.

Mertens scrutinised Nick's battered face.

'I forecast that you'd have an interesting time in Alexandria. In fact, from what I've learned, you seem to have a good time everywhere.'

'What on earth are you doing here, Colonel, if I may ask?'

'In Alex or this bar? Same reason for both, as it happens – the handover of his ship tomorrow.' He nodded at de Herdt. 'I'm filling in as military attaché at our embassy for a couple of months. Belgium and Egypt are working closely together nowadays.'

'And are your family with you in Cairo?'

Mertens hesitated. He put down his glass and looked Nick straight in the eyes.

'No, they've stayed in Beirut. Teresa's schooling is paramount, and Aisha and I agreed that there was no point in disrupting it. I'll let them know that I met you.' He looked around the room with thinly veiled disgust. 'Though, perhaps not exactly where and in what condition. Now, I must leave so as to be ready for the ceremony tomorrow. All very well for this lot.' He glanced at the partying crew. 'They can drink all night as long as they make the plane in the morning.' Mertens lurched to his feet. 'Until the next time we meet, then.'

'Indeed, Colonel.'

The Belgian had been coldly formal. Of course, it might have been because of his official position vis-à-vis de Herdt.

The captain escorted the military attaché to the door, then threw himself into Mertens's recently vacated chair.

'Good, that's typical for a diplomat – early to bed. I know what, my new friend. Come back to my ship and we can amuse ourselves. I promise you I have very fine Genever but I need someone to share it with. I can't drink with the crew on board, you understand. And you're a friend of Mertens, so you must be okay.'

Nick's instincts screamed for him to reply with a blank negative, but some sly devil made him enquire.

'And where is your tugboat?'

'Ras-El-Tin, in the naval docks.'

He smiled warmly at the captain, who raised his glass to toast him. Nick only hesitated for a moment.

'Cheers, captain. Very kind of you to ask and I'd love to come. But do you think I'd be allowed in there?'

'You'll be with us – we have an Egyptian Navy vehicle, so no problem. Come on, I'll teach you how to drink Genever.'

'Always willing to learn a new skill.'

The captain shouted something in Flemish to his crew. They staggered cheerfully towards the door, arms around shoulders and waists. Outside, de Herdt waved over a white minibus and gestured for Nick to get in the back with the seamen.

When they broke out into what sounded like a traditional Flemish drinking song Nick asked what it was called.

'Rubbishtoday.'

Eventually deciphering this as The Rolling Stones' 'Ruby Tuesday', he joined in.

Armed guards waved the minibus through the raised boom at the entry to the naval base after the driver had shown a permit, and they continued along a quay to where a dark-grey tugboat was moored. The crew were still singing as they climbed the gangplank to the vessel, Nick in their midst. Over their heads, he caught a glimpse of the stern of the freighter tied up next to the tug and its port of registration.

Rostock DDR.

On board, the crew headed for the mess. De Herdt took Nick by the sleeve and led the way up to the captain's quarters. There, he poured them both substantial slugs of Genever and gestured towards a pair of leather armchairs.

'Tomorrow, this becomes the new Egyptian captain's cabin, but tonight it's still mine. So, tell me, what were you doing in the Spitfire Bar on your own?'

Nick drank some of the spirit, took a deep breath, and told a pack of lies about being deceived by a girlfriend. The captain listened sympathetically, taking in the reddening marks from the street attack on Nick's face, and poured more Genever.

'You know I don't have to believe a word of what you say. But tonight we'll be friends and I can drink with you.'

Without pause, de Herdt started on a series of lengthy narratives about delivering vessels to distant places, clearly enjoying a fresh audience.

'Surabaya, Indonesia, now that was a hell of a voyage – waterspouts, a hurricane and the crew crawling on the deck with food poisoning.'

Nick made feedback noises as the anecdotes rattled on.

When the captain halted to relieve himself, Nick cautiously pulled back a curtain and peered out. He was looking right down on to the deck of the East German freighter and, although the dock was dimly lit, he could make out sentries standing at intervals along the side of the vessel.

'Not much to see there!'

The captain, who'd silently reappeared, guided his audience back to the leather armchairs. Nick nodded and smiled as the stories continued, each one interesting in itself but cumulatively soporific.

Nick had left the curtain partly open and a while later he noticed the illumination outside brighten. Then came a low, growling, engine-like noise; it turned out to be the captain snoring. Quickly extinguishing the cabin lights, he moved to the window and heard a roar as a sand-coloured traction unit pulled up alongside the freighter.

Hatch covers were being lifted from the vessel's hold, and a dockside crane swivelled to lower chains and a large canvas sling. With the covers removed, he could see down into the hold as the chains were hooked on to a ten-metre-long, light-brown guided missile. Protected by the sling, the missile was winched out of the ship and placed on the dockside, resting on its twin rear wheels until the traction unit backed up and was coupled.

Standing well back, fingers slippery with sweat, Nick took frame after frame with the Leica. The cargo was a new version of the Russian SA-2 Dvina surface-to-air missile. From what he'd understood from Douglas, the Egyptians had never got their hands on one before. He looked in the hold again, and saw a control-unit truck, radar aerials, and at least ten additional missiles. In all likelihood, there were more SA-2s towards the front of the vessel, but the hatch covers hadn't yet been fully pulled back.

Sonorous porcine grunts and snuffles continued behind him.

He stared into the night beyond the bright lights illuminating the ship, noting that the sentry guard had been greatly augmented. Changing film rolls twice, he continued to document the unloading.

Two hours later, at 4 a.m., the last truck and missile rumbled away, the hatch covers were replaced, the extra sentries were withdrawn and the quayside was thrown into near darkness.

Nothing to do but wait. He snuggled down in the other armchair, trying to synchronise his breathing with the captain's snoring.

***

THREE HOURS LATER, HIS fitful sleep was interrupted by the arrival of a steward with warm rolls, coffee, ham and eggs.

'Here. You must be hungry so come and share this with me, my friend. We're departing for the airport at eight thirty and you will leave with us. I think the Egyptians might be surprised to find you on board when they take over the vessel.'

Nick gratefully poured himself a cup of strong black coffee, but was too tense to eat anything.

Instead, he marched down the gangplank with the rest of the crew, all too aware that he was the only one without baggage. When the minibus was flagged down at the entrance guard post he closed his eyes. After an interminable pause he heard the driver put the vehicle in gear. Peering over the shoulder of a seaman, he glimpsed a row of sentries saluting and relaxed.

The captain dropped him off on Al-Horreya in Bulkley and, with the camera and films burning in his right-hand jacket pocket, he started up Kafr Abdou to the Consulate General.

Sitting in the sun-washed waiting area, he feigned interest in an old copy of *Country Life* while grappling with the events of the night. If what he'd seen and photographed was what he believed it to be, then this could well be his last day in Alexandria.

'You know this is heavy, heavy stuff, mate.'

After his Morse transmission detailing the missiles he'd asked the vice-consul to destroy the codebook and lose the transmitter. They were walking in the rose garden and he'd just explained what he'd seen and done.

'Could issue you with an emergency passport here in another name, but it wouldn't have your visa and residency stamps – that would cause problems at the airport in Cairo. So best you use your own. I'll send Said for you in the Land Rover in half an hour and he'll take you straight to the embassy. Okay?'

'Sure.'

Although the morning was not yet particularly hot or humid, beads of sweat appeared on Col's well-shaved upper lip.

'Better to leave the films here though, while you get your passport and things together.'

'Sorry, not on.'

'Don't understand what the issue is, old man. Just give the films to me and I'll stick them in the safe. Said will pick you up in thirty minutes. Much safer that way.'

'No, Col, I'll hang on to them.'

'Your call, sunshine. And what a way to go, if I may say so.'

On his way down the hill, Nick savoured the softness of the air and the sweet vanilla scent of freshly watered wisteria as if he were out for a morning stroll rather than his last performance on the Alexandrian stage.

He surmised that few people would be concerned when the news of his disappearance came out. To most he would just be another Bishop doing a vanishing act.

Shrill screams from the school playground rose above the hammer blows of the panel beaters in their garage by the drainage canal.

'Hamid.'

No reply.

He ran up to his bedroom, stuffed his passport into his jacket and threw a few clothes into a soft bag. On his way downstairs he paused for one last look at the back garden.

Face down on the worn wiry grass, patched with dull-red earth, lay Hamid and the boab, wrists tied behind their backs. Two soldiers with loosely slung automatic rifles stood over them.

He crept down into the sitting room. Spidery black hairs ran down the arms resting on his high-backed chair.

'*Ahlan wa sahlan!* Welcome!'

A tall uniformed figure rose and turned to face him.

'Abdul?'

'Captain Abdul to you.'

'Of course.'

'So this is where your *rehearsals* took place, is it? I believe that is how they were described.' The officer's voice was icily distant.

Only then did Nick take in the disordered state of the room. Books lay scattered across the floor, his desk drawers hung half-open and pictures were stacked against the wall.

'What's this all about? What right do you have to ransack my house? And why on earth are my servants tied up? The consul general will certainly make a diplomatic protest. This is an outrage.'

Abdul strode across the room towards him and stood uncomfortably close, chest-to-chest. He stared down. The sweet musky smell of his after-shave filled Nick's nostrils.

'You are in no position to make threats, Dr Hellyer. You are under arrest for espionage.'

Two soldiers emerged from the kitchen and relieved him of his bag, passport, camera and films. Marched out of the house, he witnessed Hamid and the boab being cast into a military truck further up the street.

An open desert-camouflaged jeep pulled into the kerb and he was forced in, a soldier on either side gripping his arms. Abdul swung himself into the front seat beside the driver, leaned back and put his feet up on the dashboard. As the jeep pulled away, Nick caught the familiar horn blast of the consulate Land Rover arriving to pick him up.

Salt-laden winds buffeted his face. As the jeep took that long beautiful curve all the way around to Fort Quait Bey, he became more and more certain of his destination.

His arrest had to be Samy's doing, surely. Bad luck, of course, that the person who'd been tasked with his arrest had turned out to be Leila's fiancé. But, after all, as an officer, Abdul was bound to have a code of honour.

On arrival at the dock gates he'd so recently passed through in the opposite direction, he was handed over to

two blue-uniformed guards and marched to a cell in the
naval prison.

Abdul followed.

'Strip.'

He obeyed.

'Put this on.'

Abdul handed him his galabeya.

'Look straight ahead.'

A camera flashed.

'Sideways.'

More flashes.

The guards left the cell with his clothes and he was left
alone with Abdul. The assault was brief and brutal, leaving
him curled up in pain on the floor. He lay in the darkness,
failing to control his breathing, and his mind from racing
ahead.

Once the films had been developed it wouldn't matter what
he told them. All that would matter would be how he was
treated before they killed him. He started a wish list: death
by drowning, hanging, beating, starvation or shooting. He
thought he preferred the latter, but suspected they might
not. After all, though, it was peacetime and he was a British
citizen. Surely they couldn't just disappear him.

He wrenched his mind back to the present and tried to
assemble facts. He was on the floor of a cell in a prison facility
in the naval headquarters at Ras-El-Tin. However, Abdul was
an army captain, so why had he been the one to arrest him?

When the guards had deposited him in the cell, all he'd
taken in was a metal chair and table and a barred observation peephole in the door. Now, underneath him, he felt the
rough texture of the flagstones and smelled the sour stench

of urine. The cell was windowless but in the darkness he could make out a thin sliver of daylight from the corridor under the door.

Later, the heavy silence was fractured by a shriek echoing down the corridor. He crawled closer to the door, made out the sound of blows before each subsequent scream. The cries ceased as suddenly as they'd begun. Straining, he heard speech but was unable to catch the words.

Then he could.

A begging refusal. '*La!*' 'No!'

A deeper shouted. '*Aywa!*' 'Yes!'

The screeches that followed went on and on. He curled up by the cell door, his ears full of the galloping irregular beat of his heart.

He felt his way back across the floor, located a front chair leg and slowly pulled himself up on to the seat. He closed his eyes.

He woke when the blinding ceiling light came on. The door was flung open. Two guards marched in and grabbed him by the arms.

As the men dragged him roughly along the corridor, he snatched a sideways glimpse through a half-open cell door. Lying on the floor was a hooded man, his back criss-crossed with vivid red scars, trousers pulled down to his ankles and a familiar pair of *shibshibs* on his feet.

The guards, sensing his momentary hesitation, half-lifted him off his feet and propelled him to the lavatory. He was strangely grateful to them as they stared blank-faced at him through the open door while he squatted and emptied his bowels because their destination hadn't been a wall and a firing squad. When they frog-marched him back, the door in the corridor was closed.

He was flung back into his cell. Abdul half-lolled in the chair, his long legs stretched out in front of him, one ankle crossed over the other. Displayed on the table were a rough canvas hood, a long wooden baton, a Leica, a sketchbook and an open envelope with dollar bills spilling out of it. Apart from the hood and baton, the other objects were all too familiar.

'Take off the galabeya and put it on the table.'

As the guards took up their positions on each side of the cell door, he stood naked in front of the captain, his hands folded over his genitals.

'So, Dr Hellyer, here we have a spy's working tools – a disguise, the means of recording military secrets and the reward for having done so. You'll also see on the table our means of extracting information from you. Have you anything to say?'

He shook his head.

'We'll soon have developed those films of yours, don't you worry. Personally, I can't wait. But first I have some questions – just as I have had questions for others already.'

Nothing he'd learned from Scottie had prepared him for this situation. He was completely on his own. Douglas had made it abundantly clear that he could expect no help.

'Samy has admitted that you rented a room at Ras-El-Tin together because you were *special friends*. Did you? Were you?'

'Yes, the bit about the room is true.'

'And the rest? He described how you wore Arab clothes and sketched him naked. He showed me one of the pictures – you do have some slight talent.'

'Yes, but that's all harmless enough, surely. You must understand how these things are. But nothing underhand at all, I assure you.'

'How sweet and touching! An English professor and his Alexandrian boyfriend.'

Abdul slowly uncoiled himself like a python awakening and preparing to wrap itself around his prey.

'I believed that your little friend was withholding information. That proved to be the case after some not-so-gentle encouragement from these two fine men.' The captain nodded in approval towards the guards at the door. 'Samy admitted you were lovers and reported that you spoke good colloquial Arabic.'

'That's not true.'

'What's not true, Dr Hellyer? Samy was Bishop's lover, so I have no reason to disbelieve that part. And Hassan, your landlord, assured my men that you spoke to him in Arabic. Oh, yes, we've had a word with him as well.'

Nick fastened his gaze on Abdul's hairy arms to divert his mind from the captain's remorseless logic.

'I wonder where you learnt your Arabic. In fact, exactly where you spent the months immediately before you came to the United Arab Republic is of great interest. But I'm sure we'll find all that out, by and by. Unless you would like to elucidate now.'

MECAS? Had to be a bluff, so he didn't reply. This, however, seemed to be what Abdul expected.

'There's more because after further gentle persuasion your little friend became most co-operative. What was it that interested you most in your walks with him? Let me guess. Was it English literature or the history of Alexandria? No, it was the docks and shipping movements. True?'

'I don't know what you're getting at.'

'Don't you, Dr Hellyer? Hassan had already told us that you'd return on your own in the evenings and roam around the port.' Abdul stood up abruptly and paced up and down the cell. 'Samy corroborated this just now and I believe him. He confessed to having followed you on two occasions when you'd gone into the dock area itself. He'd acted out of jealousy because he thought you might be seeing someone else. But he soon realised that you were there in disguise to spy on shipping, not to visit another boyfriend.'

'Yes, I've come to like your country more and more, and because of that I've done well with the language, I admit. But how on earth can there be anything wrong with falling in love with Egypt and its people?'

Abdul glanced at him, raising his heavy eyebrows as he resumed his pacing of the limited confines of the cell.

'People, oh, yes. And falling in love, that too. Assuredly you do know some interesting people, Dr Hellyer. I have learnt from Samy about your regular visits to the Consulate General to see Mr Dudley, the vice-consul, and to the British embassy in Cairo.'

'I am a British citizen and I demand consular access now. That's my right.'

A churning pain in his stomach belied the outward bluster.

'I'm sure that can be arranged.' Abdul appeared almost pleased. 'Samy has also informed us that you're a regular visitor to the DDR Cultural Centre for appointments with Dr Fussmann. Tell me, what's your interest there? Do you speak German as well, by any chance? Or perhaps you're taking lessons.' His restless prowling ceased.

Nick, eyes down, simply shook his head.

'I see. No language classes. So the question is straightforward. Are you a British or a German spy? Which?'

'Neither.'

'I further understand that your circle of acquaintances includes my fiancée, Leila.'

'Yes. You know very well we were in the same drama group.'

'But you have performed your play already, so there is no reason for you to see each other again, except in the department. Yet Hassan informs me that very recently she came to visit you in Ras-El-Tin. I wonder why.'

'Ask her yourself.'

'Trust me, I have and I believe her answer.'

'We needed somewhere to talk about two identical essays in the examination. A place where we wouldn't be overheard.'

A wild stab in the dark. A guess as to what Leila might have said.

'You and I both know that my house was bugged. The room in Ras-El-Tin was the only safe place to go to discuss the cheating.'

Abdul nodded slowly. 'Yes, cheating certainly came into it, if Hassan's account of what he overheard is to be believed. And then Samy mentioned that he had left you alone with her once at your house. Don't even bother to deny this – your boab confirmed it.'

'We were checking the examination marks and getting ready for a rehearsal.'

'I have spoken to my colleagues in Internal Security.' Abdul spoke in dull monotone, as if he'd no further personal interest in what Nick had to say and was merely reciting facts. 'They played me a most intriguing recording. It had excellent sound quality and quite graphic content. Can you guess whose voices I heard so clearly and what the people in question were doing?'

Nick stared at the objects on the table, avoiding the captain's gaze.

'Do you have anything to say? No? Are you sure? Now is the moment for you to put me right on everything.'

Abdul's flat logic was equanimity itself.

Nick shook his head without raising it. Then his hands involuntarily tightened over his groin as the captain's tone changed.

'Don't think you can take me for a fool, Dr Hellyer. I can see right through you to the dirty liar in your heart. You're also arrogantly incompetent in the extreme.' Abdul's stubby thumb jabbed him in the neck. 'You and Leila did what you did, and you later informed her it had been recorded. Of course you realised it had been – you got the consul general to complain to the governor about the listening devices.'

Jab.

'So this little episode tells me that you're lying about everything else, as well.'

Jab.

'Don't you understand? This isn't about you screwing my fiancée. It's about you screwing my country.'

'I can explain.'

'Too late. You've had your chance. Down on your knees.'

The officer sat down, nodding to the two men at the door. One came over, put the hood over Nick's head and held him from the front. The other stood beside him, smacking the baton heavily into his open palm.

'These men have delicate souls, Dr Hellyer, and therefore don't wish to see the pain they inflict. Hence the hood.'

Nick heard the swish of the baton in the air before it descended and recalled Scottie's advice to avoid blows landing in the same place and, above all, to not be a hero.

But the pain was overwhelming. Far from acting tough, he collapsed after every blow, only to be hauled back up to his knees again.

'*Khalas!* Enough!'

The guard released him with a shove so that he fell back on to the hard floor. He lay there in a curl of agony.

He heard both guards leave the cell. Then came the scrape of metal feet across the flagstones as Abdul pushed back the chair.

'Anything you want to tell me, Dr Hellyer? Is it now time for your confession?'

The hood was jerked off and he stared up at the Egyptian towering over him with the baton in his right hand.

'Yes.'

'Louder!'

'Yes, I admit I was spying for the DDR – I sold them British military intelligence. Stuff about preparations for war. I passed information I picked up at the embassy on to Fussmann.' The words – details, dates – poured out as he gazed up at Abdul. 'It was nothing against your country, you must understand. Quite the opposite.'

'So why did you spy for the East Germans?'

'All the British have done throughout history is invade, control and manipulate Egypt. I wanted to help stop this interference – to make a difference.'

'So why didn't you come straight to us with your secrets?'

'I didn't think I'd be believed.'

Despite the pain in his back, his spirits began to rise as he allowed himself to hope that his story had been swallowed.

A long silence followed as Abdul glared down at him. Then he resumed in his dull, quiet, and reasonable tone.

'That was very intelligent of you, Dr Hellyer, because you wouldn't have been believed. You're a liar through and through and, as we know from your stage performance, a very good actor. But we'll soon get the truth out of you.' The timbre of the captain's voice had become harsher. 'The beating you've just received was official – from the State. This one is personal.'

Abdul forced the hood back over Nick's head and the baton fell. Nick tried to roll into a ball but this exposed his spine and lower back. The blows came repeatedly around his kidneys until he passed out.

***

HE SWAM SLOWLY BACK to consciousness on hearing two voices speaking Arabic.

'Thank you so much. Very realistic screams. *You* should have acted in the play, not him.'

'Anything I can do to help, as always. You know – just ask me.'

'Of course. You've been most useful to us.'

Abdul and Samy.

'Hey, are you listening, Hellyer? Say goodbye your *habibi*, to your darling Samy.'

The door crashed shut and he was alone. Betrayed by Samy, who'd had the last laugh.

***

HE WOKE TO KEYS rattling, the thump of the guards' boots, and other, lighter footsteps.

'Here he is, gentlemen. The spy Hellyer. And on the table, the evidence.'

Abdul spoke in English.

'Can he hear us?'

Nick recognised Hans's voice immediately.

'Oh, no need to be concerned about this one – he won't be talking to anyone soon. Or maybe never.'

'I see.'

'However, he has confessed to spying for the DDR – a most serious matter. What he claims seems true, as the pictures in front of you on the table were indeed taken with one of your excellent cameras. So what do you say?'

'As I have already told you, my friend, yes, he *was* working for us. You can check how we passed his information on to your people. But we have no knowledge whatsoever about these photographs.'

'No?'

'Think, please – they show Russian missiles that have been transported to Egypt on a DDR ship. Why should we want to photograph them? We supplied and shipped them to you, so why would we need these pictures?'

'In that case, why would a British spy who was working for you use a Leica?'

'What you are suggesting is not consequent. If I can say something safely, you know very well in which country you have spent the last six weeks. As for the camera, I can permit myself a little joke, no? Is it our fault that we make the best cameras in the world?'

'So who was Hellyer working for, then? Let's see if he can throw some light on the subject.'

The guards dragged Nick to his feet, slammed him into the chair and whipped off the hood. Abdul stood opposite him by the table. On it lay a slew of six-by-four prints – SA-2 missiles, control vehicles and radar trucks being unloaded on to the Alexandria dockside. Beside him stood Hans and his crew-cut colleague in ill-tailored matching grey suits.

'Help me! I sold my country for you. I gave you what you wanted – please save me now.'

The man with the crew cut shook his head, then nodded to the door.

'Come, Hans. Best of luck with your search for the truth, Captain, but we cannot be of assistance.'

As the Germans left, Abdul clicked his heels together and swivelled to face Nick.

'In that case, who *did* you take these pictures for?'

Nick could not fill the subsequent echoing silence. His head, usually so full of worries, ideas, options and choices, was drained of thought as he stared at the strikingly sharp images.

His photos. His camera. End of his story.

'Very well. No answer. Your friends haven't been very helpful so far, have they? Let's see if you can do better with the next one.'

The hood was forced back on and the chair removed. Nick sat hunched against the wall as time passed. He had no strategy, no get-out-of-jail-free card. But when steps entered the cell he recognised a familiar limp. Mertens.

The guards removed the hood and jerked him unceremoniously to his feet. He covered his groin with his hands and raised his head to take in the new visitor, on whom so much now depended. The Belgian was standing with Abdul. The photos on the table had been replaced by a jug of water and two glasses.

'Thank you very much for making time to assist us after the handing-over ceremony, Colonel Mertens – it is much appreciated. Now, as I've explained, we're investigating an extremely serious breach of security involving photography of top-secret military hardware here in this port.'

The colonel gave a slight inclination of the head.

'For reasons that will be obvious, I cannot show you the pictures in question. However, it is crystal clear that the only place they could have been taken from was your tugboat. Unfortunately, the crew flew out of the country this morning so I cannot question them. I am, however, interrogating this man, who I have reason to believe took the pictures.'

The Belgian shrugged and glanced at his watch.

'My question to you, Colonel, is fundamental to my enquiry. Were you responsible for giving him access to this naval base and allowing him on board the tugboat?'

'As a military attaché under diplomatic protection you are well aware that I am under no obligation to answer your questions. But on this occasion I choose to do so. My country and yours are forging a new alliance through the supply of military hardware and naval craft. We would do nothing to jeopardise this co-operation. So the answer is no.'

'Do you know this man?'

Nick fixed his eyes on Mertens, remnants of hope in his dry mouth.

'Yes, I met him a couple months ago on the *Esperia* en route to Beirut. He became friendly, perhaps rather too friendly, with my family, and that is all. The Belgian government has nothing to do with the photographs you refer to, whatever they show. I regret that I cannot explain how they were taken from the tugboat.'

Nick's voice cracked. 'Help me, Mertens. You know very well you can. For God's sake, please.'

'Captain, be so kind as to let me have a minute alone with this man.'

'If you wish.'

Abdul left the cell. The guards watched as Mertens turned, smiled thinly, then smashed his right elbow hard across Nick's face. As he fell to the floor, Mertens bent down and hissed, 'That's for Aisha.'

The colonel gestured to the guards, indicating he'd finished his business. After letting the Belgian out, the guards departed, leaving Nick lying naked on the floor. Waves of despair crashed over him until peace came.

***

SOMETIME LATER, THE CELL door clanged and he recognised a familiar pair of brogues. Resting against the wall, bent half-double with hands on knees, he raised his head and stared across the cell at Col.

'Thank you, vice-consul, for responding so quickly to my request.'

'Always pleased to help a distressed British subject, Captain. And there's clearly a problem here, if you ask me. For starters, how on earth did he get into this dreadful state?'

Something in Col's confident manner persuaded Nick that he'd detected a wink when the vice-consul had glanced over.

Abdul outlined the situation much as he had to Mertens, omitting the tugboat angle but emphasising the breach of security and the photography of top-secret military equipment. He referred to the evidence – the camera and the developed prints. His voice was level, his tone reasonable, his manner civilised.

Surely Col would see through this veneer to the vengeful animal beneath, must have noticed the livid scars and bruises on his body.

'Dr Hellyer requested a consular visit and, as always, we complied with diplomatic protocol. However, I would point out that espionage is punishable by death in this country, after conviction in a military court. So this is a matter of the utmost seriousness.'

'Quite.'

'I wonder if I might be permitted to ask you two simple questions. You are, of course, at liberty to refuse to answer.'

'Ask away, Captain.'

'What do you know of this man? And is he a British spy? The first one is more easily verifiable than the second.'

'Yes, of course I know him reasonably well and we meet from time to time socially. He's a lecturer at the university and receives a British government subsidy through the British Council. That's it.'

'And my second question?'

'I'm afraid I will not give that the dignity of an answer, Captain. Her Majesty's government does not spy on friendly nations.'

'You may of course speak to your fellow countryman for a minute or two. I will withdraw now, but the guards will remain.'

The cell door closed behind him.

'Well, matey, this is a pretty pickle and no mistake. If they do press charges, I can try to get you legal representation. However, that may not be possible with a military court, so I'll have to check that out. Of course, I can bring you some books and food – if you're not getting enough, that is.'

Catching Nick's glance towards the table, Col passed him the glass of water. He gulped it down as if it were the last drink he'd receive.

'Listen, Col, please get me out of here. We're mates, aren't we? You know how these things work. Come on, be a sport.'

He ran out of words as Col stared back at him.

'Don't know what you mean by "be a sport", I'm afraid. I'll give you whatever assistance I can and will urge the captain to treat you humanely.' Col made it sound as if he were an abandoned dog. So this was how it felt to be hung out to dry. 'Must go now.'

When the vice-consul moved over and patted him on the shoulder, Nick winced and shrank away.

'Chin up! Oh, yes, and Grace sends her love.'

Abdul entered the cell as Col left it and immediately began to prowl. Nick was still propped up against the wall and the captain paused each time he passed him.

'It is true, then, as you told me, that you were spying for the East Germans. But who else were you working for? You clearly didn't photograph the missiles on the DDR's behalf.' Without waiting for a reply, he made another circuit of the cell. 'Nor the Belgians either, I think – always unlikely that one. However, we still need to find out how you got on the tugboat. But while Colonel Mertens is clearly not your best friend, I do think he was telling the truth.'

Abdul thrust Nick's head hard against the wall, gripped his chin with his large right hand and held him there.

'But the British vice-consul, who says he knows you reasonably well, surprisingly wanted no more to do with you than he had to. I wonder why. And once we tell the British that you were spying for the DDR he'll think even less of you.' Abdul released him and continued pacing. 'So if it's not the British, who are you spying for? Not the Americans either, I think – they were of great assistance to us over Suez. Or perhaps I'm wrong. Are you an American spy, Dr Hellyer? Do you work for the CIA?'

Nick did not respond.

'You had an envelope stuffed with US dollars in your desk, didn't you? Where did they come from? Outer space?'

'The DDR.'

Abdul laughed.

'The DDR! As likely as Mars. They have even less hard currency than us. But I do know a country closer to home that's awash with dollars. Can you guess which one?'

Nick tried to shake his head but Abdul held him firm, staring into his eyes, seeking truth. Then he let go and did a slower circuit, returning to stand face-to-face with Nick.

'No? Can't guess? I think you know very well which country I mean.' Abdul spat in his face. 'Is-ra-el. You're an Israeli spy. Do you want to know what we do with them?' Abdul paused briefly and bared his teeth, though there was no humour in his face. 'We hang them up by the balls and when they've told us all they know we cut them up into little pieces and throw them to the sharks.'

Nick returned Abdul's gaze but made no reply.

'Come on, admit it, Hellyer – you're a Zionist agent.'

The captain glared at him for a long minute, then patted him gently on the right cheek. Nick remained mute.

'You will.'

Abdul left and Nick dropped on to the floor, staring down a brightly lit tunnel from which there was no exit.

So this is how it would end.

CHAPTER 11

Funchal, Madeira, 8 July 1967

VERA TAPPED HER SILVER teaspoon against the rim of the porcelain coffee cup. From her shaded terrace fringed with wisteria, the hillside dropped steeply to the toytown city centre. Oblivious to the barking of nearby dogs and the song of the skylarks high above, her attention was focused four thousand kilometres away in Alexandria.

Once Fatima had soundlessly brought her more black coffee and slices of sugarcane cake, Vera sifted through the fan of official papers before her. With a deep sigh, she pulled out a confidential telex and reread it. Anything to occupy her time until his arrival.

How damaged would he be?

> *11 June 1967. For Your Eyes Only*
> *Hellyer: No more news. Dudley's visit after arrest*
> *followed up with formal enquiries. Arresting officer*
> *no longer in post there. Naval authorities blankly*
> *deny all knowledge of NH's existence as prisoner.*
> *Serious concern for his wellbeing (vide Dudley's ear-*
> *lier report). No evidence to presume that previous*
> *NH-related activities compromised (see section on*

Treadmill). Dudley unable to act further following
sacking of former city-centre Consulate General by
medical students at start of war and currently organ-
ising evacuation of British subjects.
Captain Abdul El Salem: Working assumption that
he was chosen to arrest NH because of personal con-
nection to his fiancée (vide previous reports from
Cairo embassy on bugging of NH). Arrest preceded
the development of the covert photos, so El Salem's
initial presence most likely to be a coincidence. His
role in the interrogation ceased when, as commander
of the battery of newly arrived SA-2 anti-aircraft
missiles, he was despatched to Cairo the next day to
oversee their operational installation.
Treadmill: Still likely to be in good odour with Egyp-
tians after relaying NH's reports. GD reported prior
to war that he was still 'warm'. Recommend keeping
open option of turning him.

Yesterday's news.

With impatience, she threw the memo back on the table.
It landed among a sheaf of newspaper cuttings.

Washington Post, 6 June 1967: ISRAEL CLAIMS MAJOR
LAND AIR GAINS.

The Times, 7 June 1967: ISRAELIS THRUST DEEPER
INTO SINAI.

The Times, 9 June 1967: EGYPT ACCEPTS CEASEFIRE.

Vera abandoned her reading and strolled over to lean
against the whitewashed terrace wall. What people were
already calling the Six Day War had ended almost a month
ago. Israel had taken all of Sinai, the Gaza Strip and the

Syrian Golan Heights after a pre-emptive air strike that had destroyed ninety-five per cent of the Egyptian air force.

She stared out past the harbour in the direction of the recently opened airport; the small military jet from Cyprus would be landing in an hour.

***

Alexandria, Egypt, 5 June 1967

FOUR DAYS AFTER HIS arrest, Nick lay on the stinking stone floor of his cell. Still naked, he bore his weight on his right side. Between waves of pain came the most exquisite itching from the lacerations on his back, as if they were home to a tribe of creeping, scratching cockroaches.

Abdul had vanished after the first evening and his place had been taken by an anonymous, bearded naval officer who combined excellent English with a complete absence of humanity. The officer, clearly tasked to extract further confessions about spying for Israel, had no compunction about sanctioning further beatings. Soon his nod to the guards had been enough and Nick had unburdened himself.

He sat up and shifted gingerly against the rough wall. In the early morning, as he drifted in and out of sleep, vivid imaginings of his past life had flashed in front of him – Hamid with a laden breakfast tray, only to shimmer and vanish before he could taste anything. His boab, respectful as always, had bowed and opened the cell door, but when Nick staggered over he found it to be locked. The two men's association with him must only have brought them and their families pain, or worse.

Over the two days that had followed Abdul's disappearance, Nick had confessed to anything he thought the anonymous naval officer might be interested in, often contradicting himself almost immediately. He'd allowed fantasy to take over, and shamelessly implicated Professor Naguib and her husband as master spies, with Rachida as a trained Mossad killer. The Union Restaurant had become the nerve centre for Israeli espionage activities, and the Willi Sitte exhibition at the DDR Cultural Centre had contained coded messages in the titles of the pictures and the positions in which they were hung. Each confession was assiduously noted and became the topic for further questioning.

He soon realised that he'd nothing safe left to give, having admitted most of what he knew and invented much more. He'd given them enough 'evidence' for a dozen show trials, so resorted instead to repeating the same fictions.

In the heat and horror of the interrogations, memories of past places and events became as real to him as the filth of his cell.

As a three-year-old, when he'd crawled into the attic of their Victorian house, the heavy door had swung to, imprisoning him in a damp, sooty, cobwebby darkness. Eventually his cries had been heard and he'd buried his tear-stained face in his mother's apron.

Now his mind had become that house and its scary attic the hiding place for his great secret. When the interrogator's questioning dragged him close to the stairs and the attic, he passed them by as if they didn't exist. In this way, he'd concealed the fact that the information passed on in his double-agent role to Fussmann had been dictated by London.

Time blurred, reality escaped his grasp and hallucinations dogged him. He saw himself dancing naked, spinning and floating through the air. Images of Leila swam into his mind – her flaming ascension as the toilet window blew out and she flew upwards, clinging to the rocket-like incinerator.

He screamed, 'You'll be burned.'

But she had been burned.

And perhaps beaten into submission, with Abdul still intent on marrying her so that his family would not know what had happened. He'd forever hold the shame of her infidelity close to him while he simultaneously thrust her away.

Then the interrogation ceased.

He knew he should have been scratching lines on the cell walls to mark the passing of time. But what was the point? He wasn't the Count of effing Monte Cristo.

The wounds on his back showed no signs of healing and he longed for them to be cleansed, as much as he desired absolution from guilt and failure for himself.

He was becoming one huge suppurating sore. The Egyptians weren't going to shoot him; they were just going to let him rot away until he died.

He missed the interrogator. Really missed him. He had some lovely stories to tell him. Some lovely bunches of coconuts. South Sea Island music filled the cell and he reached out towards the grass skirts of the dusky maidens. Parting one of them he came face-to-face with Grace and put out his fingers to touch the curves of her eyebrows, the bow of her earlobes and the firm lines of her neck and shoulders.

Different Graces floated past him as he heard her laugh turn from a ripple to a cackle. Images of this mercurial woman, blonde hair blowing out of a car window and the clearest of gazes, held desperation over his plight at bay while awakening memories of the gentlest, yet most assertive, of touches.

**

6 June 1967

E XPLOSIONS SHUDDERED THROUGH THE stone floor, rattling the metal cell door. Shocks from the blasts ran through his body, jerking him awake in terror as possible causes flickered through his consciousness.

Bombs, mines, grenades, an artillery bombardment?

Total blackness meant this had to be the middle of the night.

Sirens wailed. Not the rhythm of soft music, poetry, singing or dancing so it couldn't be one of his dreams.

Unless it was a fantasy SAS rescue mission. Unlikely. He slumped back to the floor.

The blanket of silence returned, but he couldn't sleep and lay wide-eyed until evidence of the grey dawn crept under his cell door. Left alone aside from the guards' visits with food and water, he dozed off again in the late morning.

Shouted commands, heavy-booted feet stamping in the corridor, and cell doors slamming awoke him.

The following days and nights were punctuated by screams from interrogations in the surrounding cells.

He lived through these sessions as if he were the subject of all of them – the cries of agony filling his head, his back flinching in sympathy with every blow.

He waited his turn, sure in the knowledge that they'd come for him.

But they did not.

***

20 June 1967

I N THE EARLY EVENING, as he scraped the last of the beans from his bowl, two guards flung open the cell door and forced on the hood, tightening it so he could barely breathe.

In his shocked and weakened state he was unable to keep up with their pace as they marched him down the corridor, so between them they half-dragged him, head down, out into the fresh air. They grasped his arms and legs, then swung him to and fro twice like a heavy sack, letting go at the top of the second arc. He landed heavily on the back of an open truck whose engine roared as it sped over the cobbles.

He was carried up clanging metal steps and cast forward on to a hard, unforgiving surface. He passed out.

Later he became aware of a rumbling accompanied by regular vibrations. Having tried and failed to work off the hood, he relapsed into a feverish stupor.

Jerked into consciousness by strong arms and manhandled to his feet, he swayed when the hood was taken off, and fell against the side of the lifeboat under which he'd been dumped. But when a helping arm dragged over the suppurating wounds on his back, he lashed out blindly. His weak blow hardly connected and, swiftly overpowered, he was carried half-conscious below decks on the ageing Greek freighter.

Rough hands stripped and searched him, becoming gentler when they encountered his injuries. In the cool, clean blue-and-white-painted sickbay, two patient older crewmen washed him, and treated his back.

Helped into a capacious yellow shirt and orange dungarees, he was led along narrow passages and down a steep metal staircase to the mess. There, offered a meal of rice and meat, he could only swallow a few mouthfuls. The smell of the food nauseated him and the room started to spin.

He sat and leant forward, placed his elbows either side of the unfinished plate and his head in his hands. A bearded face slipped in and out of focus as he heard, but failed to respond to, the seaman's gentle but persistent enquiries.

'Who are you, my stowaway friend? Who did these things to you? Where are you from?'

The metal table, the man's uniform and the questioning brought back memories of the prison cell and the terror of more beatings. He could only utter two words.

'British Consul.'

After two days' rest and light food, rehydrated but still shocked, in pain, reticent and uncommunicative, he was helped off the freighter on its arrival in Cyprus by the chief officer.

'Got one of yours here, Giannis.'

The official from the Consular Section of the British High Commission had been waiting at the foot of the gangplank.

'Won't say a word – but looks as if he's had a hard time.'

***

Famagusta, Cyprus, 22 June 1967

'I CAN'T HELP YOU if you won't help me.'

Nick and Giannis were sitting side by side in the back seat of the consular car, like two lovers, both unsure of what the next move would be. The official was patient, but clear.

'Without proper papers I can't help you out of the docks. And without a name I can't get the papers. Now, once again, who are you?'

Nick peered woozily at Giannis, seeing first two grey curly haired heads and then one. Obscurely comforted by the familiar smell of the Zodiac's upholstery, he gave his name.

'That's better.'

Nick waited, prepared to confess to anything.

'Afraid I can't get you into a local hospital without ID or money. The High Commission can lend you some cash to tide you over. But it'll take me a few hours to get you a temporary identification document. Understand?'

'Thank you.'

'Now I'll take you to a safe haven.'

Giannis drove him to a run-down concrete seamen's hostel in the port area. Leaving him lying on his side in a scrubbed pine dormitory bed, the consular official promised to return later in the day. Nick ignored him, staring at the shadows playing on the wall while Giannis left, shaking his grey curls.

True to his word, late in the afternoon Giannis returned, flying into the dormitory with an air of excitement and mystery.

'Come on, Dr Hellyer, let's go.'

Wary, Nick sat on the edge of the bed, ready to launch himself if an attack came, sure he'd not mentioned his doctorate.

'I knew the freighter that brought you here was bound from Alexandria, so I tried to ring the consulate there. But the lines were down – probably because of the war. That's why I got in touch with the embassy in Cairo. Then all hell broke loose – to be frank, I've never known anything like it.'

Giannis gave what he must have thought was a reassuring smile, but it seemed to belie his words.

'How do you mean? I don't follow.'

'The high commissioner received a highest priority hotline call from London within the hour, and has just briefed me personally. We've been instructed to make every possible facility available to you. I don't know who you are, Dr Hellyer, but you certainly draw a hell of a lot of water.'

***

THROUGH THE WHITE NET curtains of his room in the RAF Akrotiri hospital Nick stared in wonder at streaming pink sunset clouds. Lying on his side to safeguard his cleaned and freshly dressed back, waiting for the nurse to bring supper, and with a glass of iced lemon barley water and a call bell within reach, he allowed some of the tension to flow away.

He was convinced he'd messed up big time – but, hey, better a living failure than a dead one.

As his strength recovered in the days that followed, he questioned the medical staff about what had been happening in the world during his incarceration.

'You missed a whole Middle East war.' Leah, a shining-eyed nurse, was busy washing him. 'We triumphed! Over and done with in less than a week.'

We? Not the UK surely. Israel?

***

TWO WEEKS LATER, SITTING in the sunshine in faded RAF blue-grey shirt and trousers, Nick peered up at a heavy, broad-shouldered man whose rather over-familiar, slightly patronising manner reminded him of his school headmaster.

'Excellent, Hellyer. So glad to see you're on the mend. For my sins, I'm the British High Commissioner here, and the powers that be – that is, your masters – have arranged transport for you tomorrow. I'm to provide a car to the airport and there you'll board an aircraft to take you I know not where. Always delighted to help those who' – his chin wobbled as he chuckled – 'fight in the shadows. I'm sure you'll put in a good report on your stay here. And sorry it took us a few hours to twig exactly who you were.'

Yes, tricky one that.

***

Funchal, Madeira, 8 July 1967

T HE RAF DOMINIE TWINJET communications aircraft was starting its descent from ten thousand metres as it completed its flight from Akrotiri after a refuelling stop in Gibraltar.

The only passenger was fairly sure that he wasn't hallucinating but still felt emotionally numb.

He'd survived.

But what of the others – his lovers, friends, colleagues, servants and their families, even his students? Those he'd implicated, then abandoned to a fate for which he was primarily responsible. Guilt flooded through him. They wouldn't have been in jeopardy if it hadn't been for him.

The high commissioner had told him that he'd be met on arrival, but not by whom.

Ushered politely by the flight crew into a black limousine waiting by the dispersal area to which the jet had taxied, he pondered on who could have arranged this benign kidnapping.

The grey-uniformed driver navigated the narrow twisting coast road and deposited him at the front gate of a villa high up on the outskirts of Funchal.

He was shown to a white-walled terrace at the rear of the house by a pinafored middle-aged maid. He recognised his kidnapper: a woman in a disconcertingly floral tea dress whose gravelly voice greeted him.

'Took your time, didn't you? I've been waiting half the day.'

Having accepted a cup of tea, he sank into a soft-cushioned wicker chair.

'Drink it up now before it gets cold. Great deal for us to talk about.'

Looking her in the eyes, he raised his cup in the air as if he were responding to a toast but kept his peace.

'First of all, I expect you're wondering what on earth you're doing here in Madeira. Now this villa – where, by the way, you'll be staying for quite a while – is owned by the department and precious few people know of its existence.' She waited while this prognosis sank in. 'Put very crudely, the truth is you're lucky to be alive at all. And we're parking you here because you can't live safely anywhere else for the moment. I'm only on the island until tomorrow. After that, Fatima, who showed you in, will be taking care of your every need, as it were.'

She gave a confiding grin and her voice modulated from its customary hectoring tone.

'I suppose that if you'll let me call you Nick, I'll be Vera to you. The good news is that we're all terribly proud of you, because you did far better than any of us had a right to expect – and in the most trying of circumstances. The bad news is that your light will be hidden under a bushel forever because your achievements are top secret. Furthermore, you're too hot to handle at the moment. So it's going to be a while before you can work again.' She smiled fleetingly. 'But what a wonderful place to recover in.'

Nick glanced down from the terrace to the hillside dotted with the red-tiled roofs of villas in lush gardens and interspersed with banana plantations, and loved the warmth and softness of the air on his skin. Funchal simply sang to him, and in his present state he could take any amount of cosseting. However, guilt and the enigma of his release continued to haunt him.

'But why did the Egyptians let me go? I'd confessed to everything under the sun. Except for the big lie.'

'Simple, my dear Nick. Your captors had their hands full. On the first night of the war, six Israeli frogmen who'd been smuggled into the naval harbour by submarine, mistook a dredger and a supply barge for warships and blew them up.'

'So that was what woke me. I'd hoped it was the SAS.'

'Dream on, my boy. Unfortunately for the frogmen, but not for you, they were subsequently captured. Their interrogation in Ras-El-Tin, as you can imagine, had a much higher priority than yours. Indeed, there was to be no show trial for you at all because you'd become a major embarrassment.'

'Embarrassment?'

'Because, you see, Britain and Egypt had privately forged strong diplomatic ties – despite a certain public *froideur*. Nasser's government now understood that we'd had nothing to do with the Israeli attack. Your show trial could have jeopardised this new relationship – at the very least muddied the waters, if you'll forgive me. So the Egyptians denied all knowledge and dumped you on that freighter heading for Cyprus.'

Fatima called them into dinner. At the table, Vera raised her glass of Moscatel.

'Welcome back to the human race, my clever young Nick. Victory doesn't always go to the swiftest – but you've actually won two races for us.'

''Fraid I don't get that.'

'Your first achievement was to help us persuade the Egyptians that we were on their side. Our intelligence had strong indications that the Israelis were preparing for an attack, and the Egyptians, after our involvement at Suez in 1956, had every reason to suspect that we'd be involved in this one too.'

'So, why not tell them that we weren't?'

'Things don't work in that way, I'm afraid. The Egyptians wouldn't have believed us – perfidious Albion, you know, and all of our past history with them. What we had to do was confirm their suspicions that we might be in cahoots with the Israelis, and then prove them wrong.'

'Kind of double bluff, yes?'

'Exactly. This is what the information we leaked to the Egyptians via you and your DDR contact achieved – with enough corroborating military activity to make it convincing. So they trusted us more because they knew in advance that we had no part in the attack. Believe me, this great step forward is in some part a result of your work.'

'And the second race?'

'To be honest, when we sent you to Alex we never dreamed of the coup you'd achieve with the new SA-2s. We expected low-grade intelligence and that's what you'd been sending us. Fair enough.'

There was a long pause while she stared over the terrace wall, then straight back at him.

'The SA-2s you identified were, as you well knew, the latest version, which the Egyptians hadn't possessed before. Quite simply, the older ones were unable to deal with low-flying aircraft so the Israelis could just fly in under the radar. With the new missiles, the Egyptians could knock attacking aircraft out of the sky whatever their height. Other sources have confirmed that the advanced SA-2s, which you saw landed in Alexandria, were immediately deployed around Cairo.'

'So what happened next?'

'We passed your intelligence on to the Israelis.'

'What? I thought we were on the Egyptian side.'

'Sides are difficult in diplomacy, dear boy. But your intelligence prevented a possibly much more serious Middle East conflagration – or even a Third World War.'

'Don't get me wrong. Most grateful to you for looking after me – and flattered by your praise. But no need to soft-soap me.'

'Trust me.' Her voice had hardened and he recognised the

tone used in Quinlevan's office. 'I do *not* soft-soap people. The very real danger was that, having achieved air superiority and made huge territorial gains, the Israelis would go for regime change by bombing Cairo. Had they tried to do so, in the delusion that there were no credible Egyptian air defences, their aircraft would have been blown out of the skies. With me so far?'

'Yes, Vera.'

'The resultant humiliation would almost certainly have led to an escalation. As Israel is a nuclear power, there was a very real possibility that an atomic bomb could have been dropped on Cairo. Such an action would have inevitably provoked a similar response from the Soviet Union on Tel Aviv. Then in turn, the USA, Israel's ally, would have launched a nuclear attack on the USSR. The catastrophic global consequences are easily imaginable – you follow me?'

They had coffee on the terrace, looking out over the dancing lights of the city below.

'Something I want to know. I've asked a number of people this question and have been fed different stories. Can you tell me the truth? What really happened to Bishop, my predecessor?'

Vera put down her cup.

'Well, I suppose after what you've been through you're entitled to an explanation. So I'll tell you as much as I'm able to. Bishop was working for us. Not in a junior role like yours at all – quite a different level. We'd got him alongside a very high-ranking naval officer who, how shall I put it, shared some of his interests. But when we learned that the Egyptians had got wind of the relationship, we had to get him out pronto. A local Cambridge-trained university doctor who'd been helpful to us in the past, diagnosed Bishop as having typhoid and needing to be quarantined.'

'I think I can see where this is leading.'

'The Egyptians had no wish to admit a typhoid epidemic, despite the hospitals being jammed full with three patients per bed, so they co-operated. Bishop was flown on an RAF aircraft from Alexandria to the same hospital in Akrotiri from which you've just been discharged. He made a miraculous recovery and moved straight on to Japan.'

'And was the doctor's name Naguib by any chance?'

Vera gave him a thin smile. 'That's quite enough on that topic now. Any other questions?'

'What do you want from me?'

'We want you to recover and recuperate so that you're able to resume your duties. It is indeed fortunate that you have no next of kin, so there's no one to worry about you.'

'And my duties?'

'You can forget about the Arab world. At the very least, the Egyptians will have told their fellow intelligence services about their supposition that you're an Israeli spy – there's no future there for you.'

'So bang goes the time spent learning Arabic, then.'

'Don't be so childish – it only took a couple of months.'

'But what about my academic career? That took rather longer. Up the spout as well?'

'My dear Nick.' Vera's voice was cutting. 'We both know the reasons why it would be inadvisable for you to re-enter university life in Britain.'

'But I'd hoped that little difficulty would have been forgotten about by now.'

'The police file is still open. Your future has to be with us

– and overseas. Reflect. Are you not a learning animal? Has your experience not changed you?'

He half-clenched his fists and stared down at his fingernails.

'Your stock in the service is sky-high at the moment. Don't worry – we'll most certainly find you a posting where you can exercise your undoubted skills as university lecturer as well as agent.'

'How long am I going to be here for?'

'Oh, I'd think at least a year to be on the safe side, until you've cooled off and are fully recovered.'

'So you're dumping me here for twelve months. I'll be fit much sooner than that – and dying of boredom.'

'Listen, Nick, it's not just about your health. It's about finding the right direction for you, and positioning you to take advantage of it. Right now is a good time to work on your academic profile. We can get you excellent access to journals and books via the consulate – so a divine opportunity to write that scholarly treatise you've always had in you.'

'How would you know? I may have nothing to contribute.'

'Don't be petulant. Now we also want you to learn Portuguese. Starting at once. Not to fill in the time, but because you may need to be fluent for your next assignment if things pan out as we expect. A private tutor who will come to the house daily has been arranged for you.'

'What on earth's the point? Madeira's just an island stuck out in the Atlantic miles from anywhere.'

'Because, dear boy, as a relic of empire, Portuguese also happens to be spoken all over the world: in Africa, South America and Asia. And, of course, in Europe.'

She was treating him like a child who'd inadvertently

achieved something wonderful. But he had to admit that he loved the attention. Anyway, nothing wrong with being cared for after what he'd just been through. Being an unemployed, and probably unemployable, academic in the UK suddenly seemed less appealing.

'I'm off in the morning, taking *your* plane back to Northolt. Q will be out to debrief you shortly. He'll keep in touch via the consulate – we enjoy secure communication facilities here, courtesy of our cousins.'

'Sorry?'

'Our allies across the pond have an installation high up in those hills behind you and we share the facilities.'

Nick peered back at the fleeting banks of mist swirling over the mountains.

'You'll also be pleased to renew your acquaintance with the incoming consul and his wife – taking up post quite soon, I believe. Name of Dudley.'

He surveyed the twinkling lights spread out beneath him.

'I will. That's undeniable.'